A GOOD, PROTECTED LIFE

A GOOD, PROTECTED LIFE

A Novel

Joseph Kaufman

Walker and Company
New York

First published in the United States of America in 1992 by Walker Publishing Company, Inc.

Published simultaneously in Canada by Thomas Allen & Son Canada, Limited, Markham, Ontario.

Library of Congress Cataloging-in-Publication Data
Kaufman, Joseph.
A good, protected life: a novel / Joseph Kaufman.
p.   cm.
ISBN 0-8027-1212-6
I. Title.
PS3561.A858G66   1992
813'.54—dc20   91-47915
CIP

Printed in the United States of America

2   4   6   8   10   9   7   5   3   1

for Reb Noach

Acknowledgments

Many thanks and hurrays to:

The harshest critics
my charming and lovely wife, Elizabeth
my industrious agent, Leona Schecter
my novel-smart editor, Peter Rubie

The readers
Pamela Painter, Nick Delbanco,
Grandma Lovey, Susan Israelson,
Michael Cohen, Jane Rudolph

The great teachers
Mr. Benson of Theodore Herberg Middle School,
Mr. David Huddle of The University of Vermont,
and especially Mr. Bernard Malamud, may he rest
in peace, formerly of Bennington College

The rabbis
Rabbi Shaya Cohen, Rabbi Chaim David Ackerman,
Rabbi Aaron Feldman, Rabbi Nota Schiller,
and especially Rabbi Shlomo Fryfeld, may he rest in peace,
and most especially Rabbi David Moskovitz

The cheerleaders
my parents, Howard and Nancy Kaufman,
and my kids, Ezra, Eli, and Esther

Woe to them that call evil good, and good evil;
that put darkness for light, and light for darkness;
that put bitter for sweet, and sweet for bitter!
Woe to them that are wise in their own eyes,
and prudent in their own sight!

—Isaiah 5:20–21

PART I

◆

The Dutch
Traveler

ONE

1

In November 1980, I, Murray "Muz" Orloff, abandoned my father, Charles Justice Orloff, in the Sahara Desert because he'd turned from a simple pest into a dangerous man. We'd been traveling from Jerusalem where we lived to retrieve Charlie's older brother, Daniel Podvoll Orloff, who ran away from his only daughter's funeral and who'd been missing for twelve years.

Just try and imagine this: the cold bright dawn after the sandstorm, the creamy yellow sandiness of the land stretching to every horizon, and short stubby Charlie, age fifty-four, standing outside of our red Fun-Time tent and dressed in his black pants and white shirt and black skullcap—the dress of an Orthodox Jew—his gray goatee quivering in the dry desert breeze, his hand raised in farewell as I drive off with big black Harlon Fitzwater, the detective.

Yes, just try and imagine all the guilt, tears, vows, heart-rending grief, my regrets, not to mention the tears of my mother, Vivian, sister, Louise, and brother, Max! And then try to imagine being a fat, pale, twenty-two-year-old yeshiva boy suddenly yanked away from his family and friends by a father who'd been yanking him around for years, and then being dragged across the Mediterranean, Arab countries, and the Sahara, only to realize that his father was a kook, a dangerous pest of a man. I mean, what would you do really?

But there you have it: Charlie's totally lousy character on one side of the scale of guilt and my departure with Harlon

[3]

Fitzwater on the other. Which side is more to blame? But, then, you're missing the simple narrative facts: how Charlie kicked Daniel out of the family toy business and how Daniel's only daughter Rachael subsequently passed away. How Daniel walked out of our lives and how Charlie blamed himself for everything—a searing regret that launched him on his quest for morality and God, a quest that uprooted us from our sleepy Berkshire Hills life and careened us across the United States, to Israel and alas, to the Sahara.

But, to begin at the beginning: a Saturday morning in August 1963, a couple of months before the Kennedy assassination, in a hot and dusty toy warehouse on Pecks Road in Pittsfield, Massachusetts, where, as a six-year-old, along with Louise, age nine, and cousin Rachael, age twelve, we witnessed an argument between Charlie and Daniel over the family toy business that was to spill over into their personal lives. It was the business's slow season, when everyone worked only a half day—the two ugly secretaries, the three tattooed forklift workers, the four truck drivers who always smelled of beer—and we kids were allowed to come to work with our dads and play with the dolls and games in their wholesale toy showroom, to ride the warehouse's conveyor belts, drink Coke, and punch the adding machines, to watch the truckers drag on their Pall Malls and curse.

Cousin Rachael was our leader, a skinny girl with a thick braid of waist-length hair who clubbed Louise and me with it if we didn't play what she liked—post office, spitting contests, smoking cigarettes. She was harsh and perverse and therefore fascinating, a leader who barked commands at us in her shrill voice and issued punishments like nuggies, pink bellies, or Indian rope burns whenever we disobeyed her.

On this particular hot morning, Rachael forced Louise and me to ride down a conveyor belt and pretend to be Barbie dolls. We'd just passed through the second-floor landing and were still hovering near the ceiling of the first floor. All about us stood rows of metal shelving stacked with brown toy cartons and yellow floodlights casting brownish halos everywhere. There was the hum and zip of forklifts, their exhaust mingling with the warehouse's mildew stink and, distantly,

Chuck Berry guitar music. Rachael stopped the contraption and yelled at us to sit still. I straightened to military attention and glanced into the warehouse: Father was gripping a clipboard and walking up an aisle with a beer-guzzling truck driver named Reds Guptill, Charlie who hadn't yet gone to fat but was a stocky, thirty-six-year-old man with a jet black goatee and crew-cut hair, whose thick eyebrows slanted toward his intense brown eyes and made him look like the quick-tempered man that he was. And it was just as he was lecturing Reds in his high-pitched voice, a voice that reminded me of the chesty women singers on his opera records—"I'm warning you, Reds, that truck better get to Troy on Monday morning or else you're meat"—that Uncle Daniel burst through the swinging doors that separated the showroom from the warehouse and stalked over to Charlie, Reds stepping quickly away, and waved around a piece of paper in the dull light.

Daniel, forty years old, towered over his younger brother. He was bone thin next to Father and his upper back was slightly curved—the beginning of a hunchback. Blue pince-nez were clamped to the end of his eaglelike nose; a stogie was jammed unlit into a corner of his mouth. He thrust the paper beneath Charlie's nose and growled in a tobacco-raspy voice, "Just what the hell is this supposed to be, Chuck?"

Charlie shoved Daniel's hand away. He gazed up at him, eyebrows furrowing to a V. "It's your invitation to a partners' meeting, Danny."

"Yeah?" Daniel jeered. "And since when do we ask those idiots what they think about business?"

"Those 'idiots' happen to include your father and two uncles," Charlie said.

"Don't get righteous on me, Chuck," Daniel snapped. "We both know you're not that."

"Leave that alone," Charlie cautioned Daniel in a menacing voice.

The brothers stood silently as forklifts zipped by them. Louise glanced back at me and I shook my head. I looked back at Rachael who'd dropped down to her hands and knees. She shook her head also, none of us knowing what "Leave that alone" meant.

"Danny, I want you out as president of Toys Galore," Charlie blustered on, to explain the partners' meeting. His tone was sharper now, like Daniel had hurt him and he wanted to strike back.

"So you can be president, Chuck?"

"This wholesale business is going nowhere, Danny," Charlie answered, "and in five more years it's going to be dead."

"And I suppose as president you'd make the dead come to life?" Daniel smoothed bangs of his brown hair from his eyes.

Charlie said, "I'd do exactly what I've pushed you to do a million times."

"You mean put retail toy stores in those things called shopping malls."

"Hey, I'm tired of two-percent margins and those department store managers who want you to kiss their asses before they'll buy a gross of anything," Charlie said, and glared up at Daniel as if daring him to disagree.

"So you kiss a little ass, Chuck. That's life."

"I don't want life, Danny, I want to be rich. And these shopping malls are the future of the business."

"But the rents in those places are outrageous! And then you have to hire help. You have to advertise—"

"You have to spend money to make money. Do I need to explain that? You have to be willing to take risks. The trouble with you, Danny, is that you'd rather be president than get rich. You're not a merchant."

"And I'd rather have bread on my table than go broke."

"Who's going broke, for chrissakes! Just leave me alone and I'll make you and the partners rich men."

"But I have our children to consider," Daniel persisted. "The families of these other men—"

Charlie shouted, "You fool! There won't be saltines to eat if you don't change the business."

Charlie's voice echoed off the brown toy cartons and shocked the brothers once more into silence. Daniel folded his arms across his chest, then rocked on his heels. Charlie propped his hands on his hips and stared down at the concrete floor, shaking his head.

"I'm sorry, Chuck," Daniel said, after a long pause, "but shopping malls just aren't worth the risk."

"But they are, Danny," Charlie replied, almost sadly, as if they were saying goodbye to each other for a long time.

2

The regret in Charlie's voice as he informed Daniel of the partners' meeting, as Daniel spun about and stomped out of the hot warehouse and Charlie stood alone amid the brown toy boxes and dust swirling in the shafts of light framing him and watched his brother leave, remains etched in my mind as the first time in my life that I heard a truly serious argument between adults—the type that lasts forever—an argument that was the first dent in my child's world of warmth and light. And yet my father's regret wasn't the usual bitter understanding of past life mistakes, but rather a moment where he divined the future of his relationship with his brother and whole future of our family with its sad chain of events. It was the sharp perception that he was only a pawn in the great scheme of our history and that he remained powerless to control the effects of a partners' meeting and impending coup d'état against his older brother; that he was now only able to stand still in the mildew and exhaust smells of the hot warehouse and regret the future that he'd in many ways just created, and to feel the poverty of his own soul: the selfish impulse that made him intent on expanding the business even at the expense of his brother. For, at the partners' meeting the brothers' drama unfolded exactly as Charlie's regret seemed to predict and Old Joe Orloff and his old bachelor brothers, Tuvia and Sam, the founders and present silent partners of Toys Galore, went for Charlie's shopping mall plan in a big way. They voted him president, and Daniel, upset at being overthrown, resigned. He refused all entreaties to stay on as vice-president. And no matter how much my mom badgered Charlie to invite Daniel back into the business—Vivian with

[7]

her shoulder-length, dirty-blond hair, which she flicked away from her blue eyes with her skinny wrist, who was a head taller than Charlie, four years younger, and sixty pounds lighter, who wore bright cantaloupe-tinted lipstick, smoked menthol cigarettes, and did yoga, my mother who spoke with a Brooklyn accent and who'd been married to my father for ten years, ten years of bickering with Charlie, or we with him, years of trying "to bulldoze away the acres of your father's rough spots." No matter how much she bugged Charlie to make amends with Daniel, Charlie refused and sneered, "No way, Viv. Danny comes back if he wants but I'm not inviting him back. The man's got to show accommodation."

But Daniel never went back to work for Toys Galore. Perhaps he stayed embarrassed at being demoted. Perhaps he didn't want Charlie as a boss or to work as hard as the mall business demanded. Because as soon as Charlie took over the company, he began working fourteen-hour days and sleeping away from home. He traveled constantly to Springfield, Albany, and Troy to supervise the stores he opened up in strip shopping malls, and grew crabbier and even more volatile than before. The work paid off though, and Charlie expanded the chain to eastern Massachusetts, Vermont, Connecticut, Rhode Island, and New Hampshire.

Yet in direct proportion to how things improved for Charlie, they worsened for Daniel. He couldn't find a job: the Berkshire economy was never great, and my uncle was unwilling to move. And in a year's time, his wife, Estelle, and he sold their house and rented a mousy apartment in a low-class part of town. Ultimately, Daniel accepted a job from a friend to manage a hardware store, but no longer did we follow Rachael around the Toys Galore warehouse on Saturday mornings or see her at the occasional Sunday brunch our families had shared: the night of the bloodless coup, as my mother called it, ended any civility that had existed between our clans.

And then in March 1968, six years after Charlie's coup, the drama from the brothers' shopping mall drama unfolded yet again when Rachael, age seventeen, died of a heroin overdose. According to the local newspaper, Rachael's boyfriend at the time had given her the lethal injection. But I remember the night Rachael died and Old Joe called Vivian, and how I felt my child's world again pierced sharply as I listened to my mother break the news to Charlie at the store in Providence. I tried to imagine Rachael dead, her quiet body and pale cheeks, her braid of hair coiled onto her chest and line of dignified mourners shuffling past her bier—my re-creation of Queen Guinevere's funeral from a television movie. For this was my first death, and since I had as yet no experience with hysterical weeping or how people yanked out their hair and threw themselves on the ground—real grief—my cousin's death inspired me with only bland surprise. I half-expected Old Joe to call us back and say the whole thing was a joke or he buried her himself and we needn't trouble ourselves to drive up.

The Tuesday morning of the funeral broke clear and cold. Charlie and Vivian loaded us kids into our new '68 Chevy Impala convertible for the twenty-minute drive north to Pittsfield. The heater was broken and our smoky breath fogged the windshield. Charlie commented irritably, meaning the car, "I just bought this damned thing," and refused Louise and me the radio. "Your cousin's dead. You can do without the Rolling Stones." At the same time, Mother was explaining to Max, age six, what happened to people after they passed away. "They . . . they . . . enjoy themselves, dear," Mother said uncertainly, her foggy breath floating into Charlie's ear as she twisted in her seat to face Max. She hadn't worn her usual Day-Glo lipstick, and I noticed wrinkles from her cigarette smoking twitching about her mouth when she spoke.

"So how do they enjoy themselves?" Max asked, Max who still wore his Batman cape around the house. "I mean, I know they start off in the ground, right?"

"Right." Mother pursed and bit her lips as she thought of an answer. "Then the soul begins to rise—"

"Bunk!" Charlie blurted out. "Stop feeding the kid bunk, Viv! Tell him about the coffin and how dark it is inside—you make death sound like a love affair."

"And don't forget the maggots," Louise, age fourteen, said, grinning, her mouth flashing silver from her braces.

All the while Charlie drove up Route 20, past brown fields and red cowsheds, Shaker Village and its square buildings and round stone barn, the Eaton paper plant with its soot black smokestacks and red brick buildings, past the cedar and pine stands of the flat Berkshire Hills that was its backdrop. The sun was bright but heatless. Thin white clouds, like streamers, scudded through the blue sky. We drove by Broad Street, the turnoff for the Reform Jewish Temple, and motored up North Street, past the dilapidated row of mom-and-pop stores, Pittsfield General Hospital, past Waconah Park—the home of a Boston Red Sox farm team—and turned left into the Pittsfield Cemetery.

A short man in a black coat directed us up a right-hand fork, over a hill of crucifixes and another rise to an entourage of parked cars: a pearl-tinted hearse, a pair of black limousines, the small caravan of friends' cars. Charlie parked the new green Impala behind another sedan, the last in the line.

We walked across the yellow, frozen cemetery grass to join the burial. The crowd of mourners watched us approach. Louise and I tagged after Charlie, who trailed Vivian, who held Max's hand. Ladies' headscarves flapped in the raw wind, like kites. The tremulous rabbi's voice described life as a cruise ship that people cheered out to sea. The great irony was that no one should cheer the boat when it returned safely to port—our eternal rest after worldly cares.

The crowd of mourners was large: men in London Fogs gripping the elbows of their wives who were dressed in camel-hair coats. Some ladies wore furs; I smelled perfume. All about us rose granite and marble tombstones.

Uncle Daniel wore sunglasses and stood near the open grave, his graying hair rising and falling in the wind. His hands were thrust deep into the pockets of a brown mackintosh. His back was more curved than I remembered it and made him seem as if he were slouched over the open hood of a car, peering in as if to repair things. On the other side of the grave, by Rachael's casket, Aunt Estelle wept. Her arms were folded across her sheepskin coat. Her running mascara stained black lines down her cheeks.

"A sweet girl, a girl devoted to her parents," the clean-shaven rabbi was saying.

"There wasn't one goddamn thing sweet about that girl," Louise whispered to me.

"A girl in the bloom of womanhood, a girl on the threshold of life . . ."

I felt embarrassed by my aunt's emotion and watched my mother stare zombielike at the velvet-draped coffin. Charlie tapped a heel of his loafers against the yellow glass. He adjusted the knot of his mint-colored tie while Max bit his nails.

"And let us pray for the repose of this child's soul," the rabbi crooned. "And may her parents and family be comforted among the mourners of Zion and Jerusalem everywhere. Let us together say, Amen."

"Amen," the crowd said.

The rabbi waved a gloved hand and the blue-overalled cemetery workers stepped from behind the crowd. They began winching Rachael's casket into the ground, like lugging toy boxes from a Toys Galore landing platform into a truck. I stood near the grave and heard the men softly calling directions to each other, "Don't let go of your end yet, Jim" and "Make sure she's even." They grunted as they shoveled dirt into the open hole. Their steamy breath gusted upward, like car exhaust, as the rabbi chanted kaddish and began reciting Psalms.

Daniel peeled away his sunglasses and leaned forward over the backs of the diggers, to inspect his daughter's burial. Then he pushed bangs of hair away from his reddened eyes and stepped backward over the frozen grass, hesitantly at first, as if he needed to leave the cemetery for some half-remembered errand. After a moment, he turned quickly and hiked toward the cemetery gate, long strides like a speed skater. The crowd of mourners watched him go: a thin stooped Ichabod Crane hiking past a hillside of gravestones, past a grove of tall, leafless elms swaying in the chilly wind.

"And just where the hell does he think he's going?" Charlie mumbled to himself, but Aunt Estelle heard him from across the grave.

"He's going to get away from you, Charlie," she said, loudly, so the crowd of mourners heard her. "You screwed him six years ago when you kicked him out of the business—*his* business. You kicked him out and watched him fall down and you did nothing, Charlie. Nothing!" she shrieked, eyes bulging, her cheeks mascara-black from her tears. "Opening your toy stores and building yourself a new house while your brother has to sell his! Your daughter in private school while your niece goes on dope—" Estelle tried spitting at Charlie, but the wind only dribbled it down her chin and she stood frozen by the grave in the bright sun and glared at Charlie as the diggers kept burying Rachael.

I was only eleven but knew what "You screwed him" meant. I saw how my father's harshly cut goatee and recently longish hair, his stocky body in his expensive trench coat all quivered as he turned his back on Estelle. And I saw how he gazed with intense regret after his older brother, the same regret that I'd noticed years before in the toy warehouse, a regret that was again beyond his ability to affect, like the weather, as Uncle Daniel vanished from our lives, past the frozen yellow grass and line of parked cars, over a hill of tombstones to the chanting of Psalms.

TWO

1

Charlie stood still on the cemetery grass as the gravediggers shoveled in dirt and the crowd of mourners hurried to their cars. He stared at the hill where Daniel vanished, intent as an Indian scout, as if trying to divine clues to his brother's whereabouts. Estelle wept in her sheepskin coat, body-shaking heaves. Her sister Ina and a funeral parlor man cradled her elbows and guided her into a limousine.

The entourage of cars began pulling out. Five minutes later, there was only my family and the gravediggers in the cemetery. Mother, Louise, Max, and I watched Charlie stand with his arms at his sides and his legs together, Marine-like, his gaze riveted in the middle distance at the tall elms and tombstones on the hill where Daniel disappeared. He might have stood there a long time, too, in the sun and wind with the rest of us quiet and wanting to be respectful, but one of the gravediggers straightened, sliced his spade into the pile of tan dirt, and offered his co-workers and Charlie cigarettes. "Wanna smoke, fellas?"

Charlie came out of his trance. He peered at the blue overalled men, a confused lost look, like he'd been rudely woken from a bad dream, and he only shook his head and began trudging toward the car. We trudged after him, piling into the Impala.

Charlie drove slowly away from Rachael's grave. He followed a narrow access road by the cemetery's Jewish section and its section of crucifixes to its front entrance where he turned onto Waconah Street. A hundred yards later, he braked the car in front of the Waconah Street Pub.

"Muz, run into that bar and see if your uncle's there," Charlie told me, himself again.

Mother said, "Charlie, I hardly think Daniel would be drinking at a time like this."

"Muz, get going," Charlie said a second time, and rested his arms on the steering wheel. "And Vivian, you shut up."

I jumped out of the backseat and raced across the sidewalk. I opened the bar door and waited for my eyes to adjust: a bartender scrubbing glasses, a woman eating a sandwich. I trotted back to the Impala, hopped in the backseat, and said, "He's not there."

Charlie said, "But maybe he *was* there, Muz. Did you ask the bartender?"

"No."

"And why the hell not?" he exploded, pounding the steering wheel.

"I'll go back," I mumbled, but Charlie gunned the Impala back into traffic. He frowned as he leaned over the steering wheel, peering around North Street for his brother.

"Everybody on the lookout for Daniel," he commanded us. After another minute, he stopped in front of another bar. "Get in there, Muz," he said, voice full of threat and menace. "And this time *ask*."

But Daniel wasn't in that bar or the next one either, or any of the restaurants after that. He wasn't loitering on a park bench or trying to hitchhike out of town, and we knew he hadn't walked home because Charlie idled the Impala a block away from Daniel's house while I sneaked across neighbors' lawns and past the funeral parlor limousines to peek into his windows. Charlie grew upset then, an agitation that lasted the rest of the afternoon, replete with his thin-lipped frown, small brown eyes darting in all directions, and barking at us in his high-pitched voice. We were used to this treatment— Mother called it his Hitler mode—and we just did as we were told or gazed silently out the car windows. I was surprised that Estelle had so gotten to him. I mean, was there anything she'd said about Daniel and Toys Galore that he hadn't known? And, then, surely Charlie considered as ridiculous her accusation that Rachael's death was somehow his fault.

But when we arrived home at dusk—the western sky still pink, a sliver of moon hovering above the maple trees surrounding our house—Charlie pulled into the garage, and his black mood remained. He told the rest of us to go inside, then sat in the Impala in the approaching dark. And I began to realize, even at age eleven, that it was not only possible but probable that Estelle's recriminations were news to him. And as Charlie sat there hour after hour (Mother yelled out of the garage door from time to time for him to come inside and once donned a coat and sat in the car with him) I understood how a man could be so wrapped up in himself or his work or both that he couldn't consider those around him, but to the point of harm.

And while I didn't think Charlie completely guilty of this, he, however, did, and Estelle's bitter tirade—maybe it was the way she yelled at him in front of the mourners or the simple fact of Rachael's death—pierced him like a sharp knife. It kept him holed up in the Impala long after Max went to bed and Louise and I had put on our pajamas. It made him stomp into the kitchen later that night and announce, "She's right."

"Who's right, Charlie?" Vivian asked from the breakfast table, where she wrote a condolence note to Aunt Estelle and Louise was helping me with my math.

"Estelle's right. What she said to me in the cemetery." Charlie was almost gay, like people on TV who found Jesus.

"What Estelle said to you in the cemetery was mourner's nonsense," Mother cut in sharply, dropping her pen on the table. "First of all, Daniel left Toys Galore of his own free will. And for her to say Rachael's death was somehow your fault . . . how can you believe a thing she says, Charlie? The woman just lost her daughter for godsakes!"

"But if I hadn't ousted Daniel as president he never would have become poor and taken Rachael out of private school," Charlie said. "Rachael wouldn't have gone to public school where she met that scum Raymond who gave her the drugs."

"Please, don't make this into another ego trip, Charlie,"

Mother said, "thinking that you're the grand cause of everything."

"And what do you expect me to think, Viv?" Charlie asked, lifting his arms in a shrug.

"I expect you to mourn your niece's death. I expect you to invite your brother back into the business, though it's been six years."

"So you *do* think the business was the cause—"

"I never said any such thing." Mother shook her head violently. "You know that I always thought you were wrong not to *invite* Daniel back into the business."

"And Rachael's death is a consequence of that wrong—my wrong," Charlie declared.

"And you are impossible to reason with," Mother said.

"And real boring to listen to also," Louise said, sighing, her arm draped around my shoulder, our heads bent over my math homework.

"Louise! Your father's niece just died and he's blaming himself," Mother said. "Please try and understand."

"Yeah, yeah, I know Dad's niece just died and that he's blaming himself," Louise said impatiently, glaring at Charlie, "but I'm tired of trying to understand *him*. I want him to try and understand *me*—a teenager with acne. I mean, he's the father, dammit. It's his job! But he's always so . . . so . . . busy with himself. And those moods of his that we're supposed to live with just because he's the father and makes the money. Well, I'm sick and tired of it. We all are. If he feels so much damn remorse for Rachael, let him prove it. Let him do something to help other people for a change."

Charlie stood quietly in the middle of the kitchen, stroking his goatee. His silence wasn't absentminded, like this morning in the cemetery. Rather, from the events I've described—Charlie's argument with Daniel about Toys Galore and Rachael's death—he seemed to have drawn whatever philosophical conclusions were necessary for determined action, and Charlie was nothing if not a decisive man. Still, these events alone might not have propelled him to action were it not for Louise's speech, a disapproval that silenced him and forced him after some moments to admit, "Louise is right, too," a speech that made him turn away from us and open the garage door again—I figured he was going for another thought session in the Impala—and call back to us, a disembodied voice in the dark March night, "I swear to you all that I will change."

2

And Charlie did change, working fewer hours and spending more time at home and, later at night, volunteering for charitable causes: raising money for the United Jewish Appeal, going door to door for the Jimmy Fund, counseling teenage boys about drug abuse. Toys Galore was on the verge of big success, and for Charlie to suddenly shift gears seemed proof of his vow to change. Yet, at bottom, this flurry of domestic attention only derived from his disgust at the misery the business had caused. "If we would have been civilized, Danny and me, who knows? Rachael would be alive today and we might have gotten rich anyway." Charlie sighed, like the corporation itself had murdered her. And even if that wasn't remotely true, Charlie's enjoyment of the growing success of his business was ruined, but ruined to a degree that he spoke of selling out and becoming a shoemaker, which, ironically, threatened to revert Toys Galore into the two-bit operation that originally led to his falling out with Daniel.

Nevertheless, and despite his admirable program of good works, Charlie remained the irritable, volatile man he always was, and this bothered him greatly. "My schedule has changed but I haven't," he complained to Mother one night after he drove a troop of Girl Scouts around on their annual cookie sale. "I mean, I yelled at a Girl Scout tonight. Can you imagine that, Viv? I reduced the poor girl to tears. Tears! I felt so awful that I bought all of her cookies." He looked sadly at Mother. "I'm really a danger, aren't I, Vivian?"

"You're not a danger, Charlie. Ho Chi Minh and Fidel Castro are dangers. You're just unusually selfish."

The two of them stood in our living room with the deep-pile white rug and console television, the vases of dried eucalyptus smelling like cough drops, the charcoal sketches of hobos on the redwood walls, the upright piano that was never touched, the love seat, wicker rocker, the fireplace.

"But I'm trying to change all that by doing volunteer stuff," Charlie said, close to pleading, as if it were within Mother's power to grant him a dispensation from the worst part of himself. He still wore his trench coat as he paced about the living room. His chubby hands waved about in the air when he spoke.

"I guess that's not enough, or you're not doing the right kinds of things," Mother said, lighting a cigarette. She cocked a hand on her hip and gazed out of our living room's bay window, to think. Dark lines of sweat ran down the front of her green leotard from her yoga exercises.

"But what other charitable things can I do, Viv? Open a leper ward in downtown Pittsfield?"

"I don't know, Charlie." Mother sighed, collapsing down onto the uncomfortable orange couch. "You're the one who's concerned with his selfishness. Most of us are content to live with ours."

"But how can I be content after Rachael's death?" He circled around her on the couch.

"Perhaps what you need is therapy," Mother suggested, dragging on her cigarette, exhaling smoke that swirled in the yellow light.

Charlie swore and mock spit at the rug. "Never! I'm not going to have my thoughts sucked out of my brain by those vampires. It's like showing someone your . . . your underpants."

"But you need a structure for your thoughts," Mother added, her long graceful fingers circling in the eucalyptus-and-tobacco-scented air. "Good works alone it seems won't cure you of your selfishness."

"So how about religion?" Charlie joked. "There's structure for you."

"Yes, isn't religion just the pits," Mother agreed, tapping her ashes into the soil of a houseplant, her biting tone referring to our family's lone contact with religion, the Reform Jewish Temple in Pittsfield where Charlie sent Louise to religious school but yanked her out after one month. He thought it, "Nothing more than humanist bunk. Might as well be Unitarians, for chrissakes."

"You realize, Viv, that we hate the temple only because that rabbi is a humbug," Charlie added.

"Humbug or not, I hate the way Jewish men treat their wives. And then it's so restrictive," Mother stated shrilly.

"But I'm Jewish."

"No, you're not, Charlie. You were only *born* Jewish."

"What do you mean I was 'only born Jewish'? *I* raise money for the UJA."

"And *I* helped out on the Hadassah bake sale last year. Big deal."

"So what makes a person Jewish?" Charlie asked. "Being restrictive?"

"Something like that."

"And why do you always say, 'something like that,' Viv?" Charlie leaned against the living room's redwood paneling, his hands thrust into the pockets of his trench coat. "Don't you know anything for sure?"

"All I know is that guilt over Rachael's death and Daniel's running away is driving you batty, and that I want you to get help."

"And so why not religion?" Charlie asked, but seriously this time.

"Because it's claustrophobic, like I said."

"Bunk, Vivian. You don't know a damn thing about religion."

"But I don't care to," Vivian said from the orange couch, pursing her lips and crossing her legs ladylike, "and that seems to be the big difference between you and me right now, Chuck."

"That's only because it wasn't *your* niece who died or *your* brother who ran away," Charlie said, pacing to the middle of the living room and swiveling quickly on his heels to face Mother, legs spread in a military at-ease, his hands out of his coat pockets and waving once more through the air. "I'll tell you why you don't care about religion, Viv."

Mother sat deathly still in her sweaty green leotard and black tights. Her blond hair was pinned up from her neck, and she held the cigarette loosely between her long fingers. "Pray tell, Charles."

"Because you're a faddist," Charlie accused her, beady brown eyes trained on her. "Because life's easier that way, changing from isometrics to yoga, from the four basic food groups to just vegetables, isn't it, Viv? But don't you see that what's wrong with my Good Samaritan program is the same thing that's wrong with your vitamins: that we've only made changes of habit and not changes in character, that neither of us has a vision of one *right* way to live? And yet isn't that what I'm searching for when I drive around Girl Scouts and why you read Adele Davis books? And yet I'm still a selfish crank and you're still a faddist. We make the same mistakes again and again." Charlie stared at Vivian to make sure she understood him.

Mother nodded brusquely, crushed her cigarette into the houseplant's potted dirt, then stood from the couch, leaving a smudge of sweat on the upholstery.

Charlie went on, "I see now at least that religion has to be my next point of investigation. Judaism, Christianity, Islam—all of them at least claim absolute standards of morality, and isn't it really morality that I'm searching for?"

"And where will you start, Mr. Absolute," Mother asked. "The Carmelite nuns?"

Charlie picked at his lips. He said, "I think I'll write up a list of questions like, 'Prove to me that there's a God and what God wants of me,' and I'll take them to various clergymen."

"And who are these clergymen, Charlie? Buddhists in red sarongs?"

"Why not? The Jesuits, too. Even that humbug Reform rabbi."

"And you'll actually go, let's say, to Father Mulkeen at Sacred Heart Church?"

Charlie thought a moment. "Not at first. Since I was *born* Jewish I'll give Judaism first hearing. If the Reform guy doesn't check out, I'll go to the Conservative rabbi, and if the Conservative rabbi can't answer my questions I'll go to the Orthodox rabbi on Linden Street, whatshisname, Rabbi Mandel."

"And if there is a God, Charlie, I'm going to pray to Him that you don't drive me up a wall."

"And if I don't get good answers from the Jews, *then* I'll go to Father Mulkeen or how do you call them, gurus. And if the gurus don't check out I'll go to the Black Muslims—there's plenty of options after that. But do you hear me loud and clear, Viv? Do you hear that I'm sick and tired of living like a jerk?"

THREE

1

Needless to say, Charlie's religious plans went ahead as threatened. He met with the Reform rabbi in Pittsfield and hated him. He met with the Conservative rabbi and hated him more. His tone of voice when he reported his meetings with them was full of disgust at these men's intellectual dishonesty, a disgust so palpable that he almost refused to meet Rabbi Mandel.

"Look, what in the world is that Mandel fella going to tell me that I haven't already heard from those other two clowns?" Charlie asked rhetorically, figuring his nouveau intellectual ruthlessness would tear apart this third rabbi like it had the other two.

And yet, according to Charlie, Rabbi Mandel tore *him* apart. The old Berlin man read his list of questions, commented, "Good questions, Mr. Orloff. I wish more people would ask such questions," and then proceeded to answer "real good" to every item on his list: a God that existed and was involved in the affairs of man, who publicly gave His instructions for living, called the Torah, to three million Jews at Mt. Sinai, who created man to have pleasure and who rewarded the good and punished the bad.

"You mean you can prove that God exists?" Mother asked, as she served us Danish rolls and hot chocolate the night Charlie came home so excited from meeting Rabbi Mandel.

"Rabbi Mandel's contention is that he only has to prove it fifty-one percent."

[22]

"Are you telling me that this is the end of your search, Charlie?" Mother asked. "No meeting with Father Mulkeen, no trips to Buddhist monks? Are you telling me that you want to be an Orthodox Jew?"

"It's too early to say, Viv," he said, picking the milk skin off his hot chocolate. "All I said was that Rabbi Mandel answered my questions real good and that I'm going to speak with him again."

Mother stared at Charlie, who looked into his mug. "You're serious," she said, incredulous.

"Yes, ma'am." Charlie peered up, only half smiling.

He met Rabbi Mandel again the next week. He came home with proofs of God and the literal veracity of the Torah. And while these proofs meant nothing to Vivian and never would, strangely enough they didn't seem to mean much to him either, since he spoke no more about them. Such evidence existed, I think, merely as signals to him that his search was done, as honorable reasons why he needn't visit priests or ministers or gurus. For my father simply wasn't a philosophical man. Rather, he sought a life that made practical sense and whose discipline could make him whole.

"And what happens after you talk to Rabbi Mandel next?" Mother asked, meaning, what did she have a right to expect?

"I don't know," Charlie said. "Maybe we *will* become Orthodox Jews."

His quavering voice told me that he was just as nervous as Mother, though, as if with us kids watching him and our mugs of hot chocolate throwing steam up into the kitchen's lights, it dawned on him that his ruthlessness could actually change our lives and change them forever, that his religious search had borne real live fruits and he was already contending with their taste: how far would he allow Judaism to affect our lives?

In the end, Charlie let it affect us totally. His searing regret about Toys Galore combined with his natural aggressiveness made him start attending Orthodox synagogue on Saturday mornings, turn our house kosher, and a month after that to force us to keep the Jewish Sabbath with its myriad restrictions: no television, driving cars, switching on lights, sewing, cooking, writing—any work, in short, that was considered creating.

And still and always there remained the memories of Daniel and Rachael, Rachael and Daniel—it was difficult to say which one was uppermost in his mind. Rachael was dead and Daniel never appeared again. As the story goes (as Mother told me after Estelle told her), Daniel came home the night of Rachael's funeral with whisky on his breath, cheeks smeared with blood, pince-nez broken, and saying that he wanted out of their marriage. Estelle and he had stayed together only because of Rachael and now Rachael was . . . was . . . he couldn't say it. He sat down on the front steps and wept.

He pulled himself together. Estelle agreed to the divorce—it was known theirs wasn't the happiest of marriages. Daniel, quite drunk, proved generous: the apartment was Estelle's, the bank account, everything. All he wanted was the car, a suitcase of clothes, a few hundred dollars cash. He'd call her in a few months and tell her where to mail the divorce papers. And no, he didn't yet know where he was going nor what he'd do. All he wanted was to put Pittsfield behind him forever. He tripped up the stairs, then crumpled his wardrobe into a suitcase, grabbed the Ford's keys in the kitchen, a tub of cheese spread and box of Ritz crackers, flung down his wedding band and said, "All the best, Estelle."

And while Charlie certainly knew about Daniel's bizarre midnight departure the night of his and my mother's first religious discussion in October 1968, half a year after Rachael's death and months after he began his stint as Good Samaritan, I mention my uncle's disappearance here because the particular vehemence with which Daniel rejected us all— how else could we take it?—also informed Charlie's religious quest. From the very fact that Charlie considered the moment that Daniel ruthlessly walked out of his marriage a highly lucid one, so was his own spiritual journey built upon such ruthlessness (in addition to his own natural ambition and guilt), the three factors combining to drive him both to and away from being a Good Samaritan, to finally compose his list of theological questions that he'd ask various clergymen, and whose responses, if satisfying, would almost certainly lead to a radical change of life for us all.

And while Mother and we kids could hardly be against religion since we knew so little about it, we were, however, against Father's tyranny, a tyranny that though it forced us to do the right things—clean our rooms, mow the lawn, sweep the garage—also exasperated us and made us give into his whims because we knew so well what he was so fond of reminding us: the house, furniture, even Max's Batman pajamas, really belonged to him.

But the watershed night that launched us on our moves across the States and eventually to Israel, the ancient prelude to our African trek, was the night that we first kept Shabbos, a Friday night in the middle of December 1968. We gathered at dusk—Mother and Louise in their best party dresses, Max and I in our wash-and-wear Sears suits, Charlie in his best Nehru jacket—around the dining-room table set with china, crystal, and a linen tablecloth. Father made Mother cover her hair with a doily and made us boys wear yarmulkes. Vivian lit two Sabbath candles and stuttered her way through the Hebrew blessing that Charlie transliterated onto a Toys Galore notepad. Charlie lifted a prayer book and silver goblet filled with Manischewitz, then chanted the sanctification of the Sabbath, called kiddush, in halting Hebrew and sat and drank deeply of the wine. He passed shot glasses of the syrupy stuff to us. We adjourned to the kitchen, washed our hands from a cup—Charlie prepped us during the week what to do and when—and moved back to the table. Charlie said the bread blessing, sliced, and handed out the challah. We then ate gefilte fish, chicken soup, chicken in wine sauce, sautéed peas, spring potatoes, and finally, apple pie. We warbled out Sabbath songs from photocopied sheets; Charlie told us the stories about Moses and the Children of Israel that he learned from Rabbi Mandel. The point was, this first Sabbath was a great evening for us all: an oasis from Charlie's (and therefore ours) past months of doubt, guilt, searching, despair, anger. And so when over apple pie and licorice, Mother leveled her gaze at Charlie and gave him the ultimatum, an ultimatum based on her opinion that this Yiddishkeit had gone far enough without some sort of a commitment on his part, Father only thought briefly before he answered.

Mother said, "Charlie, Sabbath is all lovely and good but what's going to become of us? I'm willing to give this Jewish stuff a try because I'm a good sport and mostly because you're such a pain in the you-know-what when you don't get your way, but you have to convince me that you're serious. You hear me, Chuck? No flaking around. Because if you're serious—really serious—then we can't stay in Richmond. There's nothing here for the kids. No kosher food, no schools, no religious friends. Rabbi Mandel's synagogue is all old men. To stay here would be half-assed and I'm no half-ass. Ponder that one, Orloff. But if you're not serious—if you're going to chuck the whole thing after two weeks—then I want you to lighten up now: television on Saturdays and bacon for breakfast. That's the choice, Charlie. And I'm sorry if I ruined your meal, but I need to know what's going on and I need to know now."

Charlie rested his silver fork of apple pie on the china plate. He closed his eyes and fingered a gold button on his Nehru coat. Mother's ultimatum meant leaving the Berkshires forever—leaving family, friends, and Toys Galore—and while he understood this I'm not sure she did, occupied as she was with keeping up with Charlie's Judaism and always keeping Charlie on an even keel. Yet Father, who had this ability to divine the grand scheme of things—or so we thought from his correct prophecy of toy stores in shopping malls—sat at the head of the table with his eyes squeezed tight, as if he were visualizing future years of orthodoxy, a life of lovely Friday nights but also one with much less money than we possessed now. Then he opened his eyes and chuckled a bit, as if the warm glow of this Sabbath evening and prospect of many more had won hands down over a life of material riches but spiritual poverty in the Berkshires, a life that would be lived in a foul temper with the ghosts of Daniel and Rachael and lived in a business that reminded him of both. Which is how and when Charlie happily announced to us, hands held high and spread wide in blessing, "Then we're moving."

It took months to hire someone to replace Charlie at Toys Galore that pleased Old Joe, Tuvia, and Sam and to negotiate an agreement to buy him out. Each of the partners in turn begged Charlie to take a leave of absence, not to be hasty and leave for good. But Charlie remained adamant about orthodoxy and leaving the Berkshires, and he forged ahead and sold our house. He scouted out another community, Monsey, in upstate New York, where he bought a new home, and he set our moving date for the third week in June 1969. All of these decisions were bridge-burners, of course, designed to hurl the family into Judaism past the point of no return, as if Charlie worried his religious zeal would weaken when life got tough later on and that he might return to the Berkshires out of cowardice and finish his days as the president of Toys Galore, God forbid.

Similarly, delegations of cousins and friends, the local board of the UJA, the Reform and Conservative rabbis he so despised, tried persuading Charlie to remain in the Berkshires by arguing that he was forsaking a prosperous business, he was an important member of the volunteer community, his kids were completely the wrong age to move, that orthodoxy was sexist, narrow, and mean. But Charlie only seized this opportunity to burn more bridges, to preach religion to his visitors and tell some of them off, most notably the two rabbis ("You guys are full of real live spiritual horseshit"), a neighbor named Richard Slivkoff ("You're the chintziest guy I have ever had the misfortune of meeting, do you know that, Dick?") and a golfing friend, Irving Sockman ("Besides the fact that you're a pain in the ass, Irving, you also cheat").

Needless to say, we Orloffs became social pariahs. Charlie was branded a nut and we were the nut's family. The kosher, Sabbaths, Rabbi Mandel's classes—everything we did Jewishly—became more important to us now that our world narrowed, and in my wilder fancies I imagined Charlie was making us into outcasts in order to give us the historical flavor of being Jews, a pogrom mentality, to prepare us for more stressful times. In reality, this painful withdrawal from normal Berkshire existence was a good segue into our major change of life, and by the time Mullen Mayflower arrived on a hot humid June Tuesday, we were eager to move.

And move we did, down, down from the Berkshire Hills to Monsey, where Charlie settled us into a puke yellow ranch house on a quarter-acre lot in a religious neighborhood of black-suited men and wigged women with passels of kids. It was a town where blacks drove dented pink Cadillacs and Jews drove dented Chevy station wagons, where Louise, Max, and I began religious day school and Charlie attended a yeshiva for beginners, where Vivian met the neighbors' wives, commiserated about children, and shopped.

In short, Charlie threw us into a right-wing religious world where men and women never mixed, men wore Amish black suits, black hats, and white shirts, and women wore dresses with elbow-length sleeves and knee-length hems. It was a world whose primary values were Torah study and saintliness and where television and a college education, abortion, men and women swimming together, the promiscuousness of America in the late sixties, were regarded as cancers.

But though the people we met were lovely, and Sabbath in Monsey really felt like Sabbath—all the Orthodox people walking through the streets, the smell of eastern European meat dishes, the melodies of the Sabbath songs from every house—the move from Richmond to Monsey remained a disorienting one, especially for Vivian. Mother missed her colonial house in Richmond, her old friends, her yoga class. And how could Charlie argue with that? And despite the fact that he found Mother a yoga teacher and took her out to kosher restaurants, Charlie failed to ease her homesickness or otherwise convince her to wait out her depression. Thus Vivian came to demand that we move though she had no illusion we'd ever move back to the Berkshires. She said merely that she wanted a different religious community, "more modern and less ghetto, please." But she also insisted on selling our new house immediately, despite the soft market. "My religiosity depends on it, Charlie," she told Father dramatically, a claim that surely hit Father where it counted, since Judaism is nothing if not a family affair. For if Mother ceased being Orthodox or, for that matter, any of us, the whole move from the Berkshires, all the sacrifices Charlie made for our new life, would sour. It was, I'm sure, the only complaint that could have gotten Charlie to agree to sell the house and lose a lot of money quickly. And though he ranted about dizzy women whose values were corrupted by American culture, Charlie caved in. He registered the house with an agency, started another set of pilot trips, this time with Mother, and decided on Cleveland. They rented a furnished apartment for a year. And in June 1970, one year after we moved to Monsey, we put our Swedish design furniture into storage, packed the Impala, now badly dented from New York drivers, and drove across New Jersey and Pennsylvania to Cleveland where we spent another year among smart religious Jews who were more professional and "less ghetto." It was also the year that I became a Bar Mitzvah boy. Yet the stock market was lousy in 1970, Charlie's investments plummeted, and he came home one night from yeshiva announcing that he'd accepted an insurance job with Mutual of Omaha in Phoenix. He refused to discuss the decision, even to answer Louise's question why he couldn't work for Mutual of Omaha in Cleveland. But since Cleveland was always rainy in addition to being less religious and less interesting than Monsey, none of us forced Charlie to come clean about his real reasons for moving to Phoenix, not even Vivian. And since Charlie was a capable man who certainly could have found a job in Cleveland had he wished, I imagined that we were moving because he was demoralized that his original Berkshire plans had fallen apart: we weren't living in a strong Orthodox community; we weren't settled in any significant way; our money had run out. It seemed to me then that Charlie's depression took the form of breaking his will to live among the religious, like Vivian had grown homesick in Monsey. And so when our money needs arose, Charlie jumped at the chance to leave the Midwest, the place where his wife exiled him and the stock market plunged, a place of horrible weather and horrible luck, and he moved us yet again, to a dreary, rent-controlled flat in the Mexican section of Phoenix.

[29]

But Charlie only stayed with Mutual of Omaha three months. He hated the daily traveling and paperwork, the unhappy reality that people bought life insurance because the salesman was gloomy enough to convince them of impending acts of God. And since he had no cash or credit and was unwilling to work for anyone else—"I'm a businessman, not an insurance hack"—Charlie was forced into manual labor: he became a house painter. It was a supreme comedown from his executive life in the Berkshire Hills but also in his religious aspirations. We kept Sabbath and we kids attended a religious day school, but our outlook vastly secularized. Max memorized baseball statistics now instead of the Bible. Louise, age sixteen, dated boys. I figured Charlie's burn-out was due to many factors: his initial overintense theological involvements and our rapid geographical moves, our bad luck with money, the drudgery of painting houses. At the same time, none of the rest of us protested our slide into secular life. Though we enjoyed orthodoxy, the old life retained its allure.

But naturally, our Phoenix life came to a head. I say came to a head because we Orloffs were naturally melodramatic people, forever running away from or abandoning each other, both physically and ideologically, and in August 1972, my second summer of painting for Charlie, this was still the rule: we'd just finished lunch at the house where we worked when Mother phoned to say that Louise and her current boyfriend, Manuel Garcia, had been caught shoplifting at the local mall. The manager of the clothing store agreed to drop charges if the kids' parents would pick them up.

Charlie and I climbed into our third-hand Ford pickup, swapped for the dented Impala, and drove the potholed road toward the mall. We passed Spanish-style houses with red roof piping, trimmed lawns, then empty stretches of brown Arizona land. "Damn you, damn you, damn you," Charlie kept cursing, and slapped the steering wheel, as if rehearsing his anger at Louise.

At the mall, he parked by Penney's and stormed into the giant department store, past its perfume counters and leather concessions. He raced by housewives wheeling children down the mall's wide corridor, senior citizens sitting beside the water fountains, and the groups of teenagers smoking cigarettes. He stormed through the Lawrence Welk music and the air's sterile coolness, which reminded me of Holiday Inn rooms.

The cashier of The Jean Company directed us to the backroom. We passed posters of smiling couples in tight denims, folded stacks of new jeans. Charlie knocked on a metal door that was opened by a sandy-haired young man wearing a blue store vest with a nametag that read, "Manager," and underneath it, "Rick Reder."

Louise and Manuel stood in the middle of the backroom, in front of stacks of brown shipping boxes. Manuel's arm looped about Louise's waist. He wore a white T-shirt, bleached jeans, and his hair was slicked back with Vaseline; a gold hoop dangled from his left ear. His parents had also arrived: a beefy, gray-haired father with a much younger wife. As Charlie and I walked in, Manuel and his father were already shouting in Spanish.

Louise's arms were folded tightly across her chest. Her lips were clenched tightly over her braces. She wore a short red dress that I'd never seen before and her face flushed scarlet as a bad sunburn when she saw Charlie. The manager explained over the Garcias' yelling, "The boy put on the jeans and your daughter put on that dress and they walked out of the store."

Charlie tapped his thighs with his fists—tense, metered gestures, as if anticipating a rumble.

Rick was saying, "I won't press charges, but I don't want them in here again."

Mr. Garcia suddenly leaped forward and grabbed Manuel by his undershirt. He rammed the boy's head into the backroom's plasterboard wall. There was a loud swack, like a baseball against a bat. The boy sprawled to the floor, groaning, and Mr. Garcia leaned over him, threatening him in breathless Spanish. Young Mrs. Garcia cracked her gum and glared at Louise—it was surely her fault that Manuel was being thrashed.

Charlie moved close to Louise. His tanned face was orange in the fluorescent light. I half expected him to ram her face into a wall, too, and I tensed. But Charlie only lifted my sister's chin with his index finger, so she'd look him in the eye. Her face was smeared with powder, eye shadow and lipstick, like Mrs. Garcia, and her cheeks flamed so red that I also felt her shame. For a moment, I thought her obvious humiliation might be enough penance for Charlie. But his grimace hardened. In a mean bark he asked the manager how much the stolen dress was.

"Thirty bucks," Rick answered, distracted by Mr. Garcia dragging Manuel by his undershirt out of the backroom.

Charlie doled out three tens. He waspishly instructed Louise, "I want you to wear that slut dress home and show your mother. You show Max what his big sister does." He stalked out of the backroom.

I followed Charlie, and Louise followed me out of the clothing store and past the other mall shops, back through Penney's and into the parking lot. There, Charlie gestured a chubby finger for Louise to ride on the pickup's bed, with the paint cans and ladders, where she held down the hem of her dress while we drove the potholed road back to town, back past stretches of brown Arizona land, the blocks of convenience stores, the neighborhoods of stucco houses. Charlie stared glumly at the road. "This isn't what I wanted for us when we moved from Richmond," he said. "I didn't want any of my kids to end up like Daniel's daughter."

"Hey, Dad, Louise is alive," I said, irritated at the melodrama of his comparison. "There's one big difference right there from Rachael."

But Charlie only slapped the steering wheel harder. "Damn you, damn you," he cursed.

"Louise is miserable, Dad," I tried again, thinking his "damn you's" meant Louise. "What the hell do you want from her?"

"No, no, no, Muz. I'm cursing myself. Don't you see that I sold out? That I compromised on all the reasons we left the Berkshires?"

"You mean, you sold out the Judaism for a job."

"The pressure of keeping everyone happy got to me," he

confessed, "and then we had our money problems. And then I'm angry I forgot that Rachael started off this same way—with the boys."

Which is when I understood that what Charlie was really mad about was that he'd become a humbug in his own eyes, like the Pittsfield rabbis, and since he moved us to Phoenix only because of his money problems in Cleveland our Orthodox conversion was somehow tainted. He was upset that our Jewishness was not an ideal pursued wholly for the family's good but was also an attempt to erase all symmetries with his brother's life. And Louise, with her good nose for Charlie's hypocrisies, probably figured it the same way. If Charlie wasn't going to take Judaism seriously, then she wouldn't either. She'd run right into Manuel Garcia's tattooed arms.

But Charlie knew this about Louise. He knew that he couldn't keep any of us Orthodox any longer in name and practice only: he needed to inject the Judaism into our guts. That meant he'd first have to inject it into his own, and was he ready for this? It would mean leaving Phoenix and moving back into a "ghetto" community. It would mean pulling himself together and preparing himself for more financial uncertainty, willing us and himself back to Judaism's right wing.

Charlie glanced back at Louise. The sight of her vainly trying to hold down the hem of her stolen dress seemed to decide everything for him. Which is most likely why he stopped cursing and declared to me as we crashed through Phoenix potholes on this scorching August day, his voice steady as a brave boat captain's going down with his ship, "Muz, I've heard that Israel is gorgeous in the fall."

3

But there was never any need for Charlie to argue with Vivian about leaving Phoenix. As soon as Mother got an eyeful of Louise in her hideous makeup and the stolen dress, she agreed to leave. Neither did they argue about Israel, since Vivian wanted to move to another American city even less than Charlie: they'd reached the end of the continent. So Charlie went ahead and signed us up on aliyah. We sold off the last of our possessions and sent off postcards to Old Joe, Tuvia, and Sam. And on a warm Sunday morning in October 1972, three years after we left the Berkshires, we began our Zionist life with a PanAm flight to New York followed by an El Al evening flight to Tel Aviv.

I watched Charlie as our plane cruised over the dark Atlantic. He nursed a Jim Beam and looked grumpy; he glowered at the black-coated Satmar Hassidim speaking Yiddish in the plane aisles. They were intense glares, reflective of inner turmoils. And because I knew Charlie approved of such religiosity and that after his stint as a house painter he shared their contempt for the secular world, I knew it actually bothered him that his sons weren't dressed in long caftans and round black hats like these men's sons and that his wife's head wasn't covered with a scarf like these men's wives. He hoped to recoup these religious losses by our emigration to Israel, however, and I knew that his commitment to the success of our radical trip was a desperate man's. And success to him meant at least the outer trappings of intense orthodoxy—black clothes, beards and sidecurls, a dank apartment in a Jerusalem ghetto. His jealousy of the Hassidim and our Orthodox recommitment were surely part and parcel of his regret that he left Monsey for Cleveland and later on that he left Cleveland for Phoenix. It was a bitter regret to judge by the severity of his glares, as if the whole worthless, empty, and vain American cultural intrusions into his family's life were only too keenly felt by him: baseball, rock 'n' roll, miniskirts, Manuel Garcia, and romantic love.

We touched down in Lod airport near Tel Aviv. The passengers applauded, a surprising noise, like landing on pebbles. The sun was sweltering as we climbed into a shuttle bus. Soldiers were posted everywhere, even women soldiers with submachine guns.

A gruff Absorption Agency official with a pompadour of gray hair met us after passport control. Eli Moskovitz marched us with our bags through the hot, noisy terminal, past groups of American tourists and Arab men in red-and-white checked kaffiyehs and their black-shrouded wives, past Swedish girls in halter tops, college students, soldiers nibbling sunflower seeds, to a cigarette-smoky office where Charlie signed more papers to complete our citizenship. Afterward, the men shook hands and said "mazel tov." Eli walked us to a taxi stand outside the terminal where we were to be driven to an absorption center in the north to spend the next six months with other immigrants learning Hebrew and acclimating. Then Charlie and Vivian would find work, we kids would start yeshiva, and everything would turn out all right—maybe.

The absorption center, called Knesset Amunim, "Congregation of Faith," was an ugly quad of cement apartments, bomb shelters, and classrooms, all surrounded by barbed wire. Our driver, a burly Moroccan named Eitan, carried our bags to our wretched apartment. He inspected the dirty bathroom, the army cots with their mildewed sheets and rusted springs. He whistled, shook his head, and called the Israeli government "a pack of kikes." He wished Charlie and us lots of luck because we'd need it.

And under duress, we moved in. We met our fellow immigrants: richly bearded Russians and skinny Iranians, a pair of chalk white Rumanian dissidents, a Danish driving instructor with the biggest, ugliest nose I have ever seen. The center's program scheduled us for seven hours of Hebrew daily in cement bunkers that constantly echoed. The program's attrition rate—could there be any surprise?—leveled out at eighty percent. People left Knesset Amunim because of homesickness, the threat of war, Israeli rudeness.

Charlie, in his usual extreme way, thoroughly enjoyed himself. He loved Israel's rugged landscapes and guttural language, the tough camaraderie of exotic men. His enjoyment was the glee of escape, I think, that he'd successfully avoided a spiritually numb life in Massachusetts and the drudgery of Phoenix house painting. His drive for truth and meaning, which always weighed heavy upon him, seemed quite satisfied with our Holy Land move.

And so when the absorption center's program fizzled to a close, we strapped our belongings to the roof of a rented car and emigrated south to Jerusalem, where Charlie, in his remorseless quest for downward mobility and talmudic wisdom, bought a cramped apartment in the Jewish Quarter of the Old City, a two-minute walk from the Wailing Wall. He purchased a dry-cleaning store on a leveraged buy-out, and we started to live, as Charlie put it, in the belly button of the universe: in the history and present harsh realities of the Holy Land's politics, wars, hatreds, and religious passions.

Day-to-day life proved more mundane: Max and I attended yeshiva, Mother ran the Old City branch of the Jerusalem post office, Louise studied for acceptance into medical school. Charlie's dry-cleaning business never took off, his Midas touch seemingly gone forever, and he was soon forced to give it back to the bank. Eventually, he accepted a government job conducting bar mitzvahs for tourists at the Wailing Wall. It was a job, curiously, that he liked and that afforded him time to learn in yeshiva and spend time with his family, that somehow allowed his guilt and remorse about Rachael's death and Daniel's disappearance to be appeased by our Jerusalem life. Finally. Perhaps this was true because we became so religious—Mother covered her hair with a kerchief, Louise and she wore modest dresses, Charlie, Max, and I dressed in black suits—and Charlie, thinking that he'd taken us geographically and spiritually as far as he could, felt somehow expiated from his past sins.

Thus for seven years we weathered three-digit inflation, terrorist worries, and the Yom Kippur War, our continually lousy money situation, the nonreligious Jews' hatred of the Orthodox, the Moslems' hatred of the Jews. There was, in fact, so much to fear in our surrounding environment that our own anxieties were dwarfed by comparison. All of which was mentally healthy for Charlie—the enemy being without and therefore not within—and what was healthy for Charlie had always proved healthy for the rest of us. We Orloffs came to feel that Orthodox Judaism in Jerusalem was a good, protected life.

This longest, quietest stage of our lives also ended, on a clear November night in December 1980, when I invited a Dutch Jewish traveler named Rolf, who I met at the Wailing Wall, home for a Sabbath meal. I remember the evening distinctly—its weather, sights, and odors—because it so changed our lives. Church lights on the Mount of Olives divided the dark ground from the still-blue sky; Muslims in drab clothes and kaffiyehs sipped muddy coffee beneath the bare bulbs of the souk stalls; Hassidic men in knickers and round fur hats, gripping the hands of little boys with long sidecurls, bustled down the Old City's sloping alleys toward the Wall.

Rolf was thin and bearded and not so clean—I almost didn't invite him home with me except that Charlie enjoyed Sabbath guests. He trailed me up the flights of steep steps to the Jewish Quarter. I led him through narrow cobbled walkways to our cramped three-bedroom apartment where I introduced him to the family. We sang the Sabbath meal's introductory songs and Charlie chanted kiddush. We washed, and he handed out warm pieces of challah. Mother served us chopped liver, green olives, then chicken soup. Candlelight wavered; brisket replaced soup.

Father pressed Rolf to eat more food, drink more wine. He talked about the Bible portion that week. We sang again. Dessert. It was then that all hell broke loose. Tall, eighteen-year-old Max stood from his chair and Rolf asked Charlie permission to stretch his legs also. He trailed Max to the living room and examined Charlie's collection of Hebrew books. He opened a family picture album, flipped some pages, and shouted, "Daniel!"

A stunned silence descended.

"Daniel who?" Max finally asked. He shoved his thick black-framed glasses up on his nose.

"Daniel Orloff. He's right here," Rolf said, excited, and hoisted the album.

The rest of us jumped up from the table. We crowded around the Dutchman who pointed to a snapshot of Daniel, captioned, "Daniel, April 1960, Chinatown, New York." Uncle Daniel was clean-shaven in the picture, his hair slicked back. You could see it had just rained. A dozen Asian children kneeled in front of him. The kids had crooked eyes, corn-tinted skin. Each was aswim in a yellow slicker, each grinned in a wet wrap. Daniel also smiled hugely, like they were his kids.

"Describe this Daniel and where you met him," Charlie asked Rolf curtly.

"I met Daniel in west Africa," Rolf explained. "In a small country named Togo. He lives with Christian missionaries in a town called Dapongo. He built them a church. He is—how do you call it?—their handyman."

"But tell me about *him*," Charlie pressed the traveler. "What does he look like? What does he talk about?"

"He is tall but has a bent back. He has gray hair and smokes many cigars. Maybe he is sixty years old."

"Fifty-seven."

"And he talks about Rachael, his daughter who died. He talks about his brother Charlie who killed her."

Vivian screamed, "Killed her! But that's a lie!"

Rolf gazed in horror at Father. "You are this Charlie?"

Charlie stared grimly at Mother. "It's him, Viv." He rubbed his fingers up and down the bridge of his hawklike nose, as if for luck.

"But why did you kill her?" Rolf asked, indignant, as if Rachael had been his friend.

"What can I tell you, pal?" Charlie answered back, sarcastic, and mad. "I had a little too much Ripple to drink and things got out of hand." Then he tapped his foot like a metronome against the tile floor. He smoothed back his wavy graying hair and adjusted the knot of his wide rayon tie. He told me, "Get this joker out of here, Muz."

I grabbed the Dutchman's elbow. "Come on, Rolf, you just asked the wrong question," and I steered him toward the front door.

"So this is Sabbath in Jerusalem, eh?" Rolf called back to Charlie. "You should be ashamed of yourself, Mr. Charlie Orloff, for killing that young girl."

"Charlie did not kill that girl!" Vivian shouted after us.

I walked back to the living room after I let Rolf out. Charlie paced back and forth across the tiles. Mother, Louise, and Max watched him.

"It's simply lunatic to think Rachael's death was your fault," Mother said. "Daniel's obviously gone nuts over the years."

Louise agreed, "Meshuganeh."

"Nuts," I added.

"He's a shmuck, Dad," Max said. "Forget him."

But Charlie refused to be comforted. The facts were that Daniel was alive and well in a Christian mission in the African bush and that he held Charlie responsible for his daughter's death. And when Charlie became agitated in a way he hadn't been since Phoenix, I realized that the twelve years between Daniel's disappearance and this Sabbath night had been but an extended waiting period for Charlie—that he always knew that news of his brother's whereabouts would track him down and that he'd someday have to face his brother again. It was as if Daniel had granted Charlie time to contemplate his sins before he, Daniel, demanded a reckoning. Because, you see, Charlie treated Rolf's news as a summons from Daniel. "It's him, Viv," he repeated grimly, like the executioner had arrived with the noose and the noose was for him, like it was truly the difference for him between going to heaven or forever rotting in hell. "I don't see any way out of it," he reasoned soberly. "I'll have to go to Africa and bring him home."

PART II

The
Abandonment

FOUR

Charlie's resolve to go after Daniel was monumental, steel-like. He visited travel agents to price flights to Togo. When he decided that flying was way beyond our budget, he borrowed atlas after atlas from the library and pored over African maps, pinpointing Daniel's town of Dapongo and tracing and retracing possible overland routes. He got vaccinated for smallpox, cholera, hepatitis, yellow fever, and typhus. He bought a six-month supply of malaria pills, a duffel bag, canteen, mess kit, flashlight, miniature gas stove, a sleeping bag. He bought a pamphlet on how to refute Christian missionaries. In short, he was more single-minded about this trip than anything since Rabbi Mandel had introduced him to religion. But his guilt about Daniel and Rachael also resurfaced, his temper and self-concern about *his* plans. He became once again a bully, yelling at Mother if dinner wasn't ready, if his shirts weren't clean, yelling at us kids if we refused to run his errands or didn't clean our rooms or sassed him back.

News of Daniel's existence wasn't earth-shaking for us kids, though. Our distinct memories of my uncle were limited to his argument with Charlie in the Toys Galore warehouse, to watching him peer over the backs of gravediggers, how he disappeared over a hill of tombstones to the chanting of Psalms. In twelve years of utter silence, Uncle Daniel had dissolved in our minds to merely a name, and these unhappy memories to an association with a period of our lives that was forever gone. We'd been too young when we left the Berkshires to appreciate Charlie's pain about Daniel and were still too inexperienced to appreciate the dynamics of grown-up families: how brothers and sisters could become estranged from each other even more easily than friend from friend.

And so with our real lack of appreciation of Charlie's position—his wonder and nervousness that brother Daniel was still alive, his corresponding resolve to seek him out and make amends—we tried our best to talk him out of the trip. Africa was dangerous and an overland route through the Sahara was even more dangerous, we reasoned. Where would he eat kosher, keep the Sabbath? How could he conscience leaving us for such a long time? He would lose his job at the Wailing Wall, and we couldn't afford the money anyway. We would miss him, Max said.

Charlie replied, "Danny's in trouble if he thinks that I killed Rachael, and he's in trouble if he's living with missionaries. What do you guys expect me to do? Let him vanish from my life a second time?" He tugged on his gray-black goatee. He folded his hands across his paunch and gazed at all of us in turn.

We were eating dinner at a meat restaurant in the heart of Jerusalem, Charlie's once-every-three-month splurge: lamb chops all around, french fries, salads with russian dressing, assorted drinks, peppers, and olives.

"Why don't you first write Daniel a letter and invite him to Israel?" Louise suggested. She was twenty-five and shed of her teeth braces and metal jewelry. She'd turned into a beauty: loose, curly auburn hair, smooth complexion, five feet seven, slim.

"And why in the world should he write back?" Charlie asked her. "The guy thinks I killed his daughter."

I said, "Then why won't he run away when he sees you?"

"Daniel's not running anywhere," Charlie replied. "The man's been stewing in his juice for a dozen years. Believe me, he'll want to give me a piece of his mind."

Plates clattered around us. People talked. Steam hissed from an espresso machine. Our waiter delivered fresh drinks. The front door opened and closed, letting in chilly October air.

"Charlie, I don't need to tell you how I hate this trip,"

Mother started, exhaling cigarette smoke over Father's head. "And it's no secret that I'm not fond of Daniel—he was a wimp about Toys Galore and I hate wimps. On the other hand, Charlie, you might be brave but you're also a nut. You get ideas into your head and get impulsive. And then, worse, you never change your mind. So I can't stop you from going to Africa—I've come to grips with that. In fact, I can't recall that I've been ever able to stop you from doing anything. And so long as we've been together you've been right: right about toy stores and that Judaism is good for us. But I just want to point out that this is different—a trip whose only goal is to say you're sorry and sorry for things that you didn't do. Well, I think that's crazy. Despite the fact that he's your brother. Despite your goal of saving a Jewish soul from the clutches of the evil Christians." Mother took a long drag on her Kool and held the smoke in her lungs. She tucked strands of her gray-blond hair beneath her paisley headscarf while the cigarette dangled from her orange lips. "So go to Africa, Chuck, and good luck. But I have conditions—things that you'll do for me: number one is that you don't go by yourself. Number two is that you speak with Rav Eliyahu," our family's spiritual adviser.

"And where will I find someone to come to Africa, Viv—hire some shvarze with a machete?"

"You'll take Muz," Vivian offered. "He's big."

At twenty-two years old, I stood shoeless at six feet three and weighed in at two thirty. But I was hardly useful for such an adventure being a fat, self-absorbed, and cowardly young man.

"Muz belongs in yeshiva," Charlie said, understanding this.

"That's right," I agreed.

"Cut it out, Charlie!" Mother slapped the table so the dishes clattered. "If you don't take Murray and consult Rav Eliyahu, then *no* Africa."

"Okay, okay." He raised his palms in surrender.

A heavy silence descended upon us all. A silence in which we understood that Charlie's Africa trip was yet another major change for the family, a change that dredged up memories of our difficult, unhappy past. And it was precisely because Charlie was willing to yank me out of yeshiva, a place Mother and he held in the highest esteem, that I finally understood and felt the extent of his vow to retrieve Daniel. I also appreciated Mother's insistence that Father not travel alone and knew there was no way on earth I could avoid accompanying him. And so I looked from one parent to another in our heavy silence and grew worried. I listened to the restaurant's buzz of conversation, kitchen door swinging open and closed, and sizzling meat, pickled vegetables. I worried at the simple physical dangers of taking a boat to Sicily and ferry to Tunis, the rest of Charlie's proposed route through Arab countries, the Sahara and Sahel to reach Togo. We could get lost, sick, robbed, detained, killed. There were the obvious difficulties of practicing Judaism, the no mean feat of putting up with Charlie when he was crazed like this.

All said and done, my worries effected nothing, of course, since my father was the sort of man who'd look you in the eye after you explained impossibilities, and say, "So what?" And yet I had to hand it to him: he was a nut like Vivian said, but he was a nut with guts. And, ever remorseless, the night after our fateful lamb chop dinner—fateful because I was drafted into the trip—Charlie and I hiked out of the Old City to fulfil Mother's second travel condition, taking a bus to the religious neighborhood of Mattersdorf to visit Rabbi Eliyahu Schor.

It was just past dusk when we reached the rabbi's apartment building. A yellow moon hung between the big buildings that flanked Panei Meirot Street. The cold air smelled of exhaust; babies screamed.

Charlie and I climbed three flights of stairs, past rusting tricycles, carriages, and beat-up dolls. A Hebrew sign on the rav's door read,

KNOCK
WALK IN
SIT

Charlie and I stepped into the apartment and sat on benches lining a tiny entrance hall. We could see into the chalk white living room where the slight old man conferred with a yeshiva boy about my age. The rav wore a long black silk coat and large black yarmulke. He sat in an easy chair behind a table of Hebrew books and tugged his thin white beard as the boy spoke.

Our turn came. The rav greeted Charlie, "*Sholom alei-chem*, Mr. Orloff." We sat on metal folding chairs across the table from him. He asked how he could be of help.

"I came to ask the rav permission to take a trip with my son to visit my brother who has been missing for many years," Charlie began, using the word "permission" because the rav's answer to his request would have the force of religious law. Charlie then described how Daniel vanished from Rachael's funeral and how twelve years later a Sabbath guest recognized Daniel's photo in an album.

The rav asked, "And you're sure the guest knew your brother?"

"One hundred percent. I questioned him closely," Charlie said.

"Forgive me, Mr. Orloff," the rav said, "but your brother sounds meshuganeh."

"My brother did have a bad marriage," Charlie explained. "His daughter Rachael was his only joy."

"And where is your brother living now?" The rav's eyes were a brilliant gray beneath the room's fluorescent light. His hands were folded in front of him on his shiny black coat.

Charlie cleared his throat and cracked his knuckles. He brushed dandruff off the shoulder of his suit jacket. "In a Christian mission in the African bush," he admitted, and flushed red. How preposterous such a trip must sound to this holy man!

"But surely this *proves* he's meshuganeh."

"Maybe," Charlie said, "but my brother is still a good man."

"And you want to travel to Africa with this young man to get him back?" Rav Eliyahu asked, unbelieving.

"Correct." Charlie's cheeks turned redder.

The rav smoothed down the front of his silk coat. He closed his eyes to think. There seemed to me no question that he was going to forbid Charlie's trip and that he only wondered how he might cool off Charlie's zeal.

"And even if I would permit you this trip, Mr. Orloff," he said after a long pause, "and I emphatically do not, who would support your family while you were away? How would you keep Shabbos, kashrus under those conditions? How could you conscience taking your son out of yeshiva for such a trip? He is young and impressionable. He could lose his orthodoxy in such an environment, God forbid. And even if you found your brother, who says that he'd return to Israel with you? After all, he's a religious Christian."

"But we are talking about my brother," Charlie said. "My Jewish brother who has been lost these many years."

"But *you* have a family to raise." Rav Eliyahu glared at Charlie with big gray eyes.

Charlie looked down at the table of Hebrew books.

The rav and I looked at Charlie.

Charlie finally said, "Would the rav mind if I asked permission from a different rabbi?"

The rav frowned and shook his head. "Mr. Orloff, you know that one may obtain permission for anything if the question is posed dishonestly enough. But please, I beg you, think of the welfare of your son, your wife, your other children."

Charlie, unaccepting, stood from his chair. He said, "I'd like to thank the rav for sparing precious time to speak with us."

The rav sighed deeply. He raised a skinny arm in farewell. The next petitioner approached.

Back on Panei Meirot Street, I trailed Charlie in and out of doughnuts of white streetlight, toward home.

"What are you going to do now, Dad?" I asked, since according to Jewish law it was now forbidden for Charlie to go to Africa.

"I'm going to ask another rabbi," he stated.

"But Rav Eliyahu said you couldn't."

"No, he didn't."

"Well, he meant to."

"And just what the hell do you know?" Charlie stopped walking and gave me one of his looks.

I could see his nose's large pores in the streetlight, the gray in his wavy hair as it spilled out of the back of his bowler, and I grew mad that he was twisting the sense of the rav's words. "I'll bet money that the rav would have forbade you to ask another rabbi except that he knew you wouldn't listen," I said.

"But the rav didn't say no," Charlie insisted, to kill my dissent. "And I'm telling you right now, Muz, that I don't want you along on this trip. You're inexperienced and naive. You'll kvetch the first time you have to sleep on the ground."

"So bully Mother until she retracts her conditions," I said glibly, hoping to provoke him to agree.

"Sorry, Muz. I promised your mother that I'd take you and so I have to take you. Regrettably. But, I'm warning you, the first time you bellyache you'll go home and you'll go alone. Is that clear?"

"Yes, sir." Hitler mode.

And sure enough, two days later, Charlie returned home buoyant from his Wailing Wall job and announced that another rabbi had permitted the trip. And though he wouldn't tell us the name of this second rav, I figured this rabbi wasn't as legally authoritative as Rav Elihayu or that Charlie posed his question dishonestly by minimizing the physical or spiritual dangers of the trip, and that he didn't want us to find him out.

In any case, the trip was on. Charlie moved into high gear and fixed October 3, 1980, two weeks hence, as our departure date. He set about arranging leave from work and leave for me at yeshiva. He reserved boat tickets, borrowed shekels, and changed the shekels into dollars. He made sure that I got my shots and duplicates of his equipment, malaria pills, that I read his pamphlet on how to refute Christian missionaries, that we arranged a fall-back plan to meet at the American Embassy in Togo's capital of Lome if we were separated.

A palpable dread pervaded my bowels throughout this entire time and gave me a bad dose of diarrhea: my sense that Charlie had committed us to a tragic, dusty doom in an Arab town or town of Africans. My gloom wasn't simply about the obvious physical and spiritual dangers of the trip, but my gut sense that there was something else rotten and as yet unknown about the whole voyage. But as my foreboding remained unfathomable and undefined, I kept my worries to myself, and the trip, alas, proceeded as scheduled.

And, soon, far too soon, Mother was serving Charlie and me our last dinner in the land: stuffed cabbage, soy cutlets, leftover Shabbos challah. And far too soon, she was standing in her bathrobe in the following orange dawn, arms folded and leaning against the apartment's doorway, watching Charlie and me zip up our duffels in the shadowy courtyard. She bent her head to his lips when we finished, and they wrapped their arms around each other. Her breath smelled like an ashtray when she kissed me. She cautioned me, in farewell, "Don't let your father be himself out there, Muz."

And then Charlie and I were hefting our duffels. We waved to Vivian with our free hands, and she waved back. And, suddenly, we'd left our courtyard and were hiking through the deserted cobblestone walkways of the Old City, climbing down the tiers of stone steps that led to the Wailing Wall. Through a military checkpoint, around a link fence to a taxi stand. A lone Mercedes waited. Charlie negotiated our fare to Haifa port. I watched the fog lights bathing the wall and its wide empty plaza in yellow light. I listened to the faraway cries of people who each night mourned the temple's fall.

Charlie and the Arab agreed on a price. The driver roped our duffels to the roof rack, and Charlie and I stepped into the cab's warm smoky insides. And soon, far too soon, we were speeding through Jerusalem's deserted intersections and around dark curves. Buildings were huge, coffinlike shadows; a yellow moon was still visible above their flat roofs. The driver stopped for a soldier and his girlfriend near the central bus station. I counted city buses parked for the night in a lot to my left. I noticed that the sky began to blue.

We spiraled down from Jerusalem, through Judean hills that flattened to plains of wheat and cotton near the sea. We drove past gaudy Tel Aviv with its pillbox architecture and Acco with its Crusader castle and coffee stands crowded with old men. We accelerated up the coastal highway north as bright trash flipped in the wind. A heatless sun pushed through weeds of clouds.

Ships wide as soccer fields and high as a gull flies lay moored with thick twined rope to steel docks jammed with winches at Haifa port. Telephone wires crossed overhead like unkempt hair. Lone birds circled smokestacks.

Charlie paid the driver. We grabbed our duffels and hiked the pier to dock thirty-eight, to a Sicilian cruise ship named the SS *Nardi*.

We presented our passports and bags to an Israeli customs officer. We climbed the *Nardi*'s gangplank and were shown to our cabin by a Thai steward: white-sprayed steel, cramped, amidships. A floor fan sprayed metallic-smelling air at our metal bunk beds.

Once again alone, Charlie and I wrapped on our phylacteries and faced southeast, toward Jerusalem, for our morning prayers. Afterward, we climbed to the *Nardi*'s topmost deck and explored its hatches, smokestacks, life boats. We examined its Plexiglas bridge and the mustached sailors manning the boat's spoked wheel and consoles of glowing dials.

Charlie and I sat in deck chairs in the stern as the *Nardi* chugged out of port. We watched Haifa recede to a skyline of white buildings, a line of steep hills, to a thin line where earth meets sky. Charlie hummed in his black two-piece suit, white shirt, sweater, and black bowler. I was dressed the same way except that I wore a fedora. Father offered me a sourball, then opened his pocket atlas to review the first stage of our trek, marked in blue felt pen: the SS *Nardi* to Sicily, a ferry from Palermo to Tunis, a train ride from Tunis to Algiers.

"Come on, Dad, this is so crazy," I said, feeling my stomach rumble.

"It sure is," Charlie said, and grinned.

And I could see with the sentiment of the world and odds of success so weighed against him, that Charlie was in his element. It was a situation he hadn't found himself in for years. He was enjoying himself immensely. And as I sat next to him, sucking my red sourball, I understood that Charlie needed such epic moral struggles to make him feel truly alive.

It was like rock climbers or mercenaries, people with danger-ous avocations. But I resented his offhand tone, "It sure is," and I resented being shlepped along on *his* epic struggle. In fact, I resented everything of the bully about him. I had for years and years; we all had. And yet my discontent on the boat was worse than usual, since, unlike our geographical moves toward Judaism, I considered the risks of this journey as outweighing its possible benefits of salving Charlie's con-science and bringing Daniel back to Israel. There was too much, in short, that was shady about the whole thing.

But now we slid westward in a gray sea, divorced from our family and Jerusalem, the tight center of our good and pro-tected life. Charlie remained in his deck chair throughout that first morning and afternoon of our voyage, reviewing his pamphlet on Christian missionaries and crunching sourballs between his good white teeth. I prowled the SS *Nardi*'s various decks, like a refugee, feeling dislocated in my black clothes and lonely among the Arab businessmen and the Italian men in their smart suits, more than anxious about all the bad that tomorrow would surely bring.

FIVE

1

My dread of Charlie's trip, best exemplified by my diarrhea and stomach cramps—Vivian packed us a bag of meatball sandwiches and fried chicken to carry us through to Palermo—was aggravated by the three days of rain and foggy weather of our passage and the SS *Nardi*'s nauseating yaws; by Charlie's constant talk about the Sahara's possible dangers and dangers of Arab countries, and by his resolve to travel through them without changing our clothes. "I don't condone apologetic behavior," he explained to me as we docked in Palermo, carried our duffels down the gangplank and into a brick hangar for Italian customs. "We go through this trip like proud men, like marines. We go dressed like Orthodox Jews." Such dread, I realized, after we pushed through the iron-mesh doors at the end of the customs building and the horde of fat, black-scarved women screamed at us, "*pensione*," and grabbed our sleeves and we hurried across a boulevard to a bistro where we sipped Cokes and killed the rest of the afternoon until our night ferry to Tunis, such dread was not some unreasoned anxiety but rather the simple strong fear of Charlie's iron will: how many dangers was he willing to overlook to pursue Daniel? It was the sort of fear that would only increase as the terrain grew more foreign, as the exotic land reflected the unchecked blossoming of Charlie's plan.

Thus, as I sensed my father's capacity for reckless bravery growing, I grew more taciturn. I stared vacantly out of the bistro's windows, at urine stains on walls, bands of crows picking through heaps of trash, at dirty pigeons on window ledges, the palsied, November arms of the boulevard trees. And I became irritated when Charlie yet again consulted his pocket atlas, reading off place names, "Ustica, Vulcano, Stromboli. I wonder what *that* place is like. What do you think, Muz? What's Stromboli like?"

"How would I know?"

"Come on, Muz, stop being a pill. You've been like this since Haifa and it bugs me. Look, I can always send you home."

"So send me," I said, not meaning it, and growing angry at Charlie's threats. They wouldn't allay my fears or inspire my loyalty. It was, of course, how Charlie operated and what I expected from him after all these years. But such threats only alienated me from him and his epic journey. They made me into more of a liability than I otherwise might have been because they made me aware of my own cowardice—that I was unwilling to say and mean it, "Fine, Dad. Leave me here and good riddance to *you*." That I stayed with Charlie only because he could take care of me physically disgusted me, and washed me in loneliness and a growing mistrust of my father's judgment. It was the sensation of being out of control and swept toward danger, like a car skidding over ice, like those dreams where you're pulled against your will over a cliff. I had, finally, the uncomfortable, practical perception that I could find Daniel more safely on my own. I say, "uncomfortable," because who wants to admit that his father's become a dangerous man?

We shlepped our duffels back through customs at dusk and climbed aboard the ferry. We settled ourselves at a torn leather booth in the lounge. The ship cast off at ten o'clock; the crossing was to take all night. The weather was again lousy, and the Arab men in drab work clothes, students with backpacks, pairs of well-dressed tourists, crowded indoors.

Charlie and I took turns reciting our evening prayers on the ferry's deck—salt spray, cold wind, utter blackness toward Jerusalem in the east. We ate tuna sandwiches and the oranges and apples we'd bought in Palermo. Charlie figured, "Three more weeks traveling, one week to find Danny, two weeks to talk him out of Jesus, and one month home." He waved his hand dismissively at the Arab men and women who stared sullenly at us and wondered aloud, "What will I say to Danny when we first meet?"

"Hello," I advised him. "You'll say hello."

"Hello Danny," Charlie practiced, trying out his best smile, a smile that made him look like he'd just thieved something. "How have the years been?"

"You'll talk with him. Buy him a drink," I said. "You'll apologize to him for Toys Galore."

"I'll apologize for Rachael," Charlie agreed dreamily, swept back a dozen years to the Pittsfield Cemetery or perhaps further to some memory of Rachael I didn't suspect.

The lounge was warm and noisy, filled with cigarette smoke. There was no place to lie down except the floor. Charlie and I spent the night sipping tea and speaking to a pair of Swedish travelers. Once in a while, I strolled the dark slippery deck of the ferry.

I kept trying to be happy.

Near three in the morning, the coast of Africa shone as a yellow twinkling diadem in the night. I followed Charlie to the bow where he gripped a capstan to steady himself. His goatee bent in the land wind that reached us. His black clothes and straight posture, his bushy gray-black eyebrows that met over his eyes, made him stern looking, like a Baptist preacher come to convert heathens.

The sea calmed. The sky lightened and cleared. We approached Tunis and docked on schedule at dawn. We breezed through customs and grabbed a taxi to the train station to Algiers. Mediterranean waves clapped the beach along the port road. The warm North African air held a scent of kelp. Tunis evolved from aluminum sheet shacks to cement homes and second-story houses surrounded by protective walls, to a skyline of eight-story buildings still rimmed in colored lights.

The small French-built train station had brick eaves and a gazebo roof. Charlie bought us sleeping berths for the overnight trip and we stowed our duffels in lockers. We walked some hours around Tunis before we left. I was in my attempt-to-be-happy state, and Charlie was excited by the great boarded-up synagogue and outdoor market where we bought pita rolls and cans of sardines, vegetables, nuts, and fruit and stopped for a Turkish coffee.

We climbed aboard the old beat-up luxury train just past noon. Our compartment was drafty and urine stenched. By midafternoon, we were crawling up the rugged Medjerda and Hodna mountains, tracks clacking like shivering teeth. We passed Constantine, Tizi Ouzou, Roui-ba—Arab villages of mud and cement huts lining rutted dirt streets. Charlie asked me, "What do you suppose is in Roui-ba?"

The next, fifth morning of our voyage, we limped into Algiers: white stone buildings anchored to small parabolas of hills, work-worn dories in a sea dark as india ink. The conductor had woken us late and we were scrambling to get dressed. The train slowed into the station; passengers were already waiting in the corridors to exit. Charlie, in only his Jockeys, reached for his money belt only to find it gone. Frantically, he searched our duffels and overturned mattresses, but there was nothing. He hurriedly dressed and checked the corridor outside. He checked the bathrooms, the eating car, and questioned passengers in broken French as they left the train. He complained to the conductor.

But there was nothing to find and nowhere to reclaim our cash—Charlie didn't believe in traveler's checks—and I was forced to hand over the few hundred dollars he'd given me in case we were separated. I assumed, happily, this would be the end of our trip—Mother certainly had no spare money to wire us. But, as usual, I grossly underestimated my father's resolve. I mean, would anyone normal trek across Africa with someone else on three hundred bucks? And yet, as Charlie stared out of our compartment's dirty window, sheets, pillows, and contents of our duffels scattered across the floor, as the conductor whipped open our compartment and demanded that we leave, Charlie only smiled and soon he was grinning, and my fragile rationalizations to hold back my dread collapsed like a worn dike: I knew that he'd decided to do just that.

I asked him crossly what he was smiling about.

"Don't you understand, Muz, that God wants to see how

badly I want to see Daniel? That He's putting this obstacle in my way only as test of my resolve?"

"You're nuts, Dad." I heard the terror in my voice. "God's telling you to go home."

"We'll hitch rides. We'll eat only bread," he planned. "We'll sleep on the ground."

"The ground?"

"We'll find jobs if we need to. We'll barter work for food, work for housing."

"This is too crazy, Dad. Mother wouldn't go for this at all."

"So go home to your mother, you baby!" He glared at me. His fists were clenched and his jaw thrust forward, like he wanted to fight.

My dread burst back upon me in one tingling rush, through fingers and toes, up and down my spine. Charlie's smile had chilled me, his explanation that God was testing him. For I understood such language, this axiomatic Jewish outlook that the proper use of the physical world was the way to heaven, that all of earth's trials and tribulations were, in fact, tests from God. And while in our case I felt Charlie misapplied this stricture, I realized with a shock that the principle seemed suddenly weird, that I didn't believe in it at all. My eyes were simply too fleshy, my attachment to physical comfort too keen. I say "shock," because to what effect had I spent all those years in yeshiva learning Bible and Talmud, keeping kosher and the Sabbath? Nothing had been internalized, I saw, no moral values had been organically grown. The whole Judaism was entirely Charlie's doing, not mine; it always had been. And as he grinned then glared at me in the smelly train, wrapped up as he was in his stark universe of God's ways and tests and me feeling the religious schism between us, I couldn't fail to be impressed with his courage at the same time that his recklessness scared the hell out of me. For while his "You baby!" shamed me into gazing at the floor, I was impressed that comfort meant absolutely nothing to him and commitment everything. I was impressed, conversely, how flabby, hazy, and gray my own religiosity truly was.

Thus Charlie and I journeyed tensely on. We hardly spoke as we restuffed our duffels and descended into the Algiers train station—steel-and-brick depot, scuffed marble floors, frosted glass wall panels—and walked past crowds of darkly dressed Arabs and police. A fellow traveler, a cheaply cologned Moroccan dandy named Hakim Nosirrom, whose cravat wiggled at his throat when he spoke, commiserated with our loss and whistled for a taxi. He took us to a bar at the southern edge of town where Algiers's green-brown plains rose into the Atlas Mountains.

We hitched a ride into the Sahara from a band of ropey-haired Rastafarians headed toward Libya to sell a dozen white Peugeots. We followed Algeria's north-south highway into the Atlas foothills to their snow-encrusted peaks, to where the land turned the brown of dried chicken bones, where thorny scrubs and sharp-edged grasses grew from bedrock. We drove through oases of square, sepia houses ringed with groves of palm trees and thick mud walls: Soul El Ghazlone, M'Sila, and El Kantara.

On Friday afternoon, at the oasis of Laghouat, Charlie and I left the Jamaicans. We prepared for Shabbos in a cheap hovel by a smoking garbage heap—ten dollars for a cool, dark room with mats, a water pitcher, and cups. We bought bananas, figs, and coconuts in the dusty souk. We bought dried red peppers which we stewed together with onions and canned sardines on our portable gas stove.

And at dusk, one week into our trip, Charlie and I lit Sabbath candles and prayed. We ate our sardine stew and fruit and, after dinner, wandered about Laghouat. I watched men wrapped in dark cotton robes, and their veiled women. The quarter-moon whitened the ground, like a dying neon bulb. The stars sparkled like shards of stained glass. Shabbos felt odd in this distant Muslim land, this vast sandy world, and especially because of the tension between Charlie and me. It was odd enough to make me feel like an anachronism, as relevant as a screen door in a submarine.

On Sunday morning, Charlie and I found a ride from an aging French beauty named Carla Ernester. She was a woman close to sixty, with the embalmed look of ladies whose loss of sex appeal is death to them: platinum hair, garish makeup, nose-withering perfume. Carla offered us a ride to Ougadougou in Upper Volta (now Burkina-Fassau), the country north of Togo, where she hoped to sell her Renault and rendezvous with her African boyfriend. In exchange, Charlie and I would push her Renault out of the sand when we got stuck.

And push we did, all the way from Ghardaia through the Grand Erg Occidental. Carla was an awful driver, and it seemed like Charlie and I were forever straining against the hot fenders of her tiny car. Our fingers blistered; skin peeled from our faces and necks. Once in a while, I'd glanced up from our pushing and watched the Sahara stretch flatly to a blue curve of sky. No vegetation, no thorns, no roots. The furnacelike sun. Horizons of sand stippled like thick egg creams. We drove by wrecked and abandoned cars, oxidized green and black, distillations of pure despair.

The Saharan plains rose to hills in the Grand Erg Occidental. The air felt like a sheet of heat. Dunes flanked the Renault, great frozen brown waves. Father and Carla drifted quickly into mutual dislike. Charlie's high school French was fluent enough to offend Carla with his right-wing politics and religion. Carla, for her part, accused Israel of Palestinian genocide. Charlie retaliated by calling the French anti-Semitic apes.

Which didn't help our cause the next Friday afternoon, after Carla's five-day scenic southwest detour through Timimoun, Adrar, Reggane, and Ain Salah. Charlie asked Carla to stop for our Sabbath and naturally she refused.

He explained that we couldn't travel from sundown Friday to Saturday night and that if she didn't wait for us we'd be stranded in these lifeless flats. Carla refused again with a Gallic "Oomph" and "Non." And who could blame her? Charlie had been abusive all week long, attacking de Gaulle and d'Estaing, the French judiciary that convicted Albert Dreyfus, Mitterand's Palestinian sympathies.

"But we are people, too, Madame!" Charlie exclaimed, arguing that in all decency she should wait for us.

But Carla remained singularly unimpressed with my dad. She touched up her platinum curls and smeared on fresh red lipstick in the sideview mirror while he ranted, and then unroped our duffels from the car's roof and pushed them to the desert floor with a thud.

"There are many truck tracks here, messieurs," she noted cheerfully, as she bent daintily into the driver's seat of the Renault that Charlie and I had pushed so well. "You should have no problem finding another ride." Then she closed its door and started the engine. She wished us *"Bon Shabbat."* And soon, racing the flats, our aging beauty was a blemish of dust.

Charlie and I didn't speak that whole afternoon as we pegged our red Fun-Time tent into the desert soil and boiled up tubers we'd purchased in Tamanrasset. Neither did we speak on Shabbos morning itself, even while we ate—the slightest tact on Charlie's part would have saved us the ride with Carla and I was angry about that.

Hot, windy late afternoon. I paced a big circle in the sand outside our tent. Charlie broke the ice between us. "You're mad at me." This was his backhanded apology for stranding us. And as I realized how fed up I was with him, and that I didn't care anymore about his previous threats to send me home alone, I called out to him, "Wow! Dick Tracy figures out that Muz is mad!"

"I said I was sorry."

"No, you didn't! You never say that you're sorry. All you do is rant and rave and bully me. I'm sick of this trip and sick of you! I'm tired that you can't keep your mouth shut."

"Cut it out, Muz. We aren't the Carlas of this world. We aren't abandoning Daniel to those Baptists in the bush."

"But Daniel *wants* to be abandoned to those Baptists in the bush."

"He will over my dead body." Charlie poked his finger into his chest, for emphasis.

And I saw yet another time how I couldn't temper my father and how dangerous he could be, stranding us here like this, and I shut my mouth, unable to listen to his rebukes and plans any longer, any of his conversation. We finished the day in silence. And it was with a great sense of relief that Saturday night I heard a car in the distance. I scrambled out of our Fun-

Time tent and waved my flashlight about—any company would be better than my dad's.

The roaring sedan was soon upon us. It slid to a stop in the sand. A grinning black giant emerged from its insides, Satan himself in paisley shorts, an untucked polo shirt, and high-top sneakers, a huge man giving off emanations and acts like he'd just bled a sheep or delivered someone of his illusions. The man laughed maniacally when he saw us. "Dr. Livingstone and his factotum, I presume." He spoke in American English, gestured toward his rusting car, a Volare convertible he called Lena, and without pause heaved our duffels into the trunk and collapsed our tent for us. Charlie and I stepped into the Volare and the big man hopped into its front seat. He gunned the engine and introduced himself as, "Harlon Fitzwater, private dick." He raced off with us into the chilly Saharan night.

2

Mr. Fitzwater drove through the night. Static from the car radio crackled in the air; dunes loomed like walls in the headlights. The giant black man (he wasn't, actually, so much bigger than me) always outflanked the sandy maze, though, like some wizard rat. He talked incessantly in his rich deep voice. He regaled Charlie and me with work stories and places that he'd been: a murder in Berlin, a kidnapping in Buenos Aires, cock fights in Thailand, opium dens in Shanghai, the beautiful Volga River, the Himalayas' blue-white snow.

I sat alone in the Volare's lumpy backseat, wondering what sort of man could gather such experience, give off such vitality. Near dawn, I had my clue. Mr. Fitzwater switched on the car's inside light and showed Charlie and me a photograph of a man named Winston Raymont. The man was in his sixties. He had thin gray hair, puffy cheeks, and the blotched nose of a drunk. He and his girlfriend, Babette Moucher, were wanted for the sabotage of a nuclear reactor in Niger, a sabotage done with plastique that killed eighty-nine and wounded fifty more. Mr. Fitzwater, a free-lance detective based in Paris, had been hired by the Niger government to track down the fugitives who were most likely holed up somewhere along the west African coast and out of the jurisdiction of the Niger police.

What I mean to emphasize, though, was the relish with which the big man described his past crime stories and his present mission of capturing Raymont and his moll, a relish that displayed his appetite for the world's physical beauty and mysteries, his raw thirst for experience. It was an appreciation that seemed to be its own reward: he asked nothing of people or the world other than that he be left alone to pursue his livelihood. Such a free life, concerned solely with its own enjoyment, was a revelation to me. It was the antithesis of my bitter traveling with Charlie and years of rabbi talks in my yeshiva about the purpose of man as a servant of God. And while such highly structured moral living had been good for me—I'd never taken drugs or had a girlfriend, both deflections from scholarly accomplishment—the blossoming of my abhorrence for my dad and my realization that Judaism was in no significant way a part of me made such living feel like a sham: praying and wrapping on phylacteries were onerous; the myriad laws concerning Sabbath observance felt like a noose. And it was not until I met Mr. Fitzwater that I realized what I'd been feeling like recently was a hypocrite. For, then, I'd never met a secular person who I admired, no grand soul who could communicate the world's excitement to me, who could prove an example and mirror to my soul.

Similarly, as Charlie sensed my infatuation with the detective—the big man offered us rides to Togo, he offered us jobs in Lome to look out for Raymont while he continued up the coast—so he bothered me more about Torah learning, about being careful with my prayers. His concern was for my spiritual well-being, of course, that the big man would undo in two weeks of traveling together what had taken him years of sacrifices to accomplish. But Charlie was not out of sorts for my sake alone. Rather, he perceived in Mr. Fitzwater a prototype of the Toys Galore life he'd rejected, a life in his opinion that was interested solely in its own aesthetic sensations, whose "Eat, drink, and be merry," philosophy considered living an inert opportunity without grand purpose, something to be used solely for personal gain, which challenged and affronted my father. Which perhaps made him feel that he, too, must justify his Orthodox life.

Consequently, the detective and my father argued about everything, arm-waving, name-calling arguments that lasted whole days and nights, from Tamanrasset where the big man picked us up through the Nigerian border town of Assamakka, where black Africa began. Politics quickly gave way to morality. Charlie accused the detective of living only for his own thrills. Mr. Fitzwater, for his side, declared heaven and hell phony. They were concepts that existed only to make people slaves to those who religiously ruled. He called this morality with a price tag. "You're pimping yourself to the lowest bidder, Chuck."

We traveled through the Sahara and into the Sahel, the semivegitative region that stretched a thousand miles to the savannahs of Nigeria, Benin, Togo, Ghana, and the Ivory Coast. The detective stopped in the uranium mining town of Arlit in northern Niger. And with the help of local police, he inspected Winston Raymont's abandoned house for clues to his whereabouts. Charlie waited in the car. I waited on Raymont's cement porch, intrigued by the Africans' basalt skin, the policemen in safari hats, turbaned Fulani men dressed in bright swatches of cloth, how infants were swaddled to their mothers' backs and how women carted sacks of dried gourds, goat hides, and bundles of secondhand clothes on their heads.

We met a witness who said that the fugitives had escaped from the reactor site into the Nigerian waste. The detective steered us off Niger's two-lane international highway, zigzagging through miles of lote bushes, sand, and laterite bedrock. No people or car tracks were visible anywhere. The air roiled with heat; the sky was blue as a cold sea. I felt a sharp loneliness for Mother, Louise, and Max here. I felt enduring shock at African poverty, that people couldn't afford medicine and babies starved, the intolerable sense of vulnerability that these people in pain could so easily be me.

I dreamed in the Volare's backseat in the hot noon of these days that Charlie and Harlon Fitzwater in arguing about life were really arguing about me: who would gain custody over my soul, who control my destiny. The dreams were nonsense yet the poignancy of choice they dramatized between my father's and the big man's lives felt very real to me. The long voyage from Jerusalem—our stops, starts, and misfortunes—had shaken my Jewish outlook. And now that I was removed from family and friends—all environmental support—my desire to leave Charlie made Mr. Fitzwater's lifestyle seem very attractive, attractive enough that it seemed an alternative to Judaism. And while I could never make such a choice with Charlie around—he'd kill me before he'd allow me to become nonreligious—the seed of my discontent, nevertheless, had been sown. The possibility of a different life than Charlie's had squarely presented itself, and I considered it.

These days of reverie ended one Thursday afternoon. We were traveling along the rocky plains when the Volare's right rear tire blew out and we skidded to a stop. The sun's fiery yellow sheen cooled to orange, to red, as Mr. Fitzwater pried off the tire and examined the large puncture, as he reached into the trunk only to find the spare had also gone flat. He sat down on the hard ground, frustrated. He leaned against the Volare's front left wheel and munched Ritz crackers and swigged from a thermos of Tang. A few minutes later, he lay down on the orange gravel. He stared at the half-moon and swirl of stars that emerged in the wide sky.

In the meantime, I boiled up millet gruel on our camp stove. Charlie pitched our tent as a strong northerly wind began to blow. After a while, Mr. Fitzwater sat upright and announced his plans. He said that we were hours away from Tanout, the closest town. The tires' rips were serious. He could temporarily patch them, but the least jagged edge, the least extra weight might repuncture them. He proposed, therefore, Charlie remain with the gear while he and I drove for new tires. I would accompany Mr. Fitzwater in case the Volare needed to be pushed from sand.

Charlie and the detective faced each other in the windy night. After their endless disagreements, this felt like the end of the ride, the dark starry parting of their ways. Only fatigue checked more arguments between them, and I suspect only the big man's need for me to push the Volare prevented him from patching the tire by flashlight and driving away, like Carla.

And though Charlie realized Mr. Fitzwater's plan could strand us in two different locales—he reminded me of our fallback plan to meet at the American Embassy in Lome—he permitted me to accompany the detective since the plan was sensible. Charlie sighed unhappily, though, glum at the prospect of being stranded once again. He emphasized to Mr. Fitzwater that the following evening was the Jewish Sabbath and I couldn't ride in a car after sunset. The big man assured Charlie that we'd return before dark. He lay down for the night then and soon was snoring next to Lena.

Charlie paced a parabola over the rocky ground and began lecturing me about my religious duties. It was his parting speech to me and he spoke impatiently, like I'd been monstrously disloyal. His fat, white hands were locked behind his back. His graying hair flew about in the cold wind. He reminded me that the purpose of life was to have pleasure in God, that such pleasure was our heavenly service, that such service was an obligation extending unto death.

"And yet who wants to die in the service of God?" Charlie asked rhetorically.

"Good question," I agreed, sitting in my white shirt, sweater, and black pants on the hard ground. My legs were crossed like an Indian, my arms folded across my chest because of the cold.

"So just what is this service?" Charlie lectured on. "God needs us to bring Him bread? He needs us to bring Him praise?"

Our red tent luffed outward then collapsed in the chilly sirocco, like lungs.

"Of course not," Charlie answered himself. "Our sages taught us that God created the world for His glory, for us to know to serve Him. That's why a person has to know what he's living for. If a human being doesn't understand deep in his heart what his purpose and meaning are in this world, then he doesn't have a prayer of a chance of getting what he wants. Such a person is a zombie."

Charlie paced back and forth over the hard ground. The detective coughed and resumed his snoring. I drew my knees to my chest for warmth. *I* was the zombie Charlie was speaking of and this irritated me.

"A person knows what he's living for by knowing what he's willing to die for."

I crab-walked to the tent's mouth to escape the wind. An animal shrieked in the desolate plains.

"Then you have the Communists and the Red Brigade, people everywhere dying for their causes," he was saying. "Do these people really believe they're going to heaven? They don't even believe in heaven! So what are they dying for?" Charlie paused dramatically. He whipped around and faced me. "Because they're dying for *meaning*," he emphasized, his voice a high-pitched Yiddish whisper. "Because meaning is what a human being's got to have. When the Almighty gave us a Torah, He was teaching us that our ultimate pleasure is meaning, Muz. That the only meaning that matters is what is eternal. Otherwise, we'll be wiped out when the sun bursts into a nova, and so what?"

I crawled into our tent; I shimmied, dressed, into my sleeping bag.

"Eternity is meaning and the Almighty is meaning," Charlie went on talking outside. "To be connected to His will is meaning. Love meaning, Muz. You need it. This is your life, not body pleasures, not tall tales. You don't have to give your life for God. You have to be *willing* to give your life. To understand that He is the purpose of our seeking and the only meaning there is, that this is our quest in this world and our job."

He still didn't realize that I was gone. What a crank! And cranks are dangerous, I thought. I shivered in my sleeping bag but felt comforted that I was to accompany Mr. Fitzwater the following morning to Tanout, that for a day I could leave my weird father behind.

The fourth Friday of our trip broke clear and hot. Mr. Fitzwater patched the tires and by midmorning we were ready to leave. Charlie gripped my shoulders. "You be careful out there with big Harlon." He gave me a kiss and hugged me close.

I took my place in the Volare's front seat—Charlie's seat—as Mr. Fitzwater switched on the engine and drove forward in the rocky plain. I turned in my seat and waved at Charlie veiled in the tires' kicked-up dust, a lone figure standing next to our abandoned duffels on the flat, gravelly land. I felt relieved to be leaving him but also nervous: it was the first time that I was truly alone with the black man and everything felt dangerous and suddenly very alive.

Mr. Fitzwater drummed the steering wheel to the languid beat of his reggae tape. He swerved around stunted lote bushes in our path, the small dunes of dry grainy dirt. We made Tanout without a hitch in four hours, yet by the time we found a mechanic with the proper tires, it was too late to retrace our route to Charlie before the Sabbath.

So the detective, as per his agreement with Charlie, agreed to spend the night in Tanout. He parked the car in front of a two story cement hotel at the far end of the village's sandy main street. The proprietor, a thin man with tribal scars gashed along his chocolate black cheeks like tire treads, swished flies from himself with a horsehair fan. He trudged up the hotel's stairs and showed us a filthy room. "Welcome to paradise, boy," Mr. Fitzwater said, and tossed his overnight bag onto a foam pad whose corners curled upward like a tea saucer. He inspected the town from the room's cracked window while I contracted the proprietor to buy me bread and fruit for Shabbos.

It was after dark that Friday night that the sandstorm began: howling wind rattling the hotel's aluminum roof sheets, waves of sand pounding the room's window. It was impossible to walk outside and I imagined Charlie huddled in our Fun-Time tent, reviewing his pamphlet on how to refute Christian missionaries, nursing his anger at me for leaving him behind.

I prayed perfunctorily. I ate my bananas and bread, and Mr. Fitzwater and I went to bed early. The storm lasted the next day and through Saturday night. The proprietor fried plantains for us when Shabbos was over and sold us palm wine. The detective entertained me with war stories, tales of spies, opera plots; we stayed up late drinking.

The next morning, the big man nudged me awake with his toe. I stood up and looked out the window: the sky its normal ocean blue, the sun already blasting the town with its merciless heat. I dressed and stepped outside. The land beyond the ratty hotel was trackless from the sandstorm, smooth as glaze.

The detective leaned against the Volare's hood, twirling his sunglasses. He looked me straight in the eye, like Charlie might. "Muz, I'm not driving back for your father."

My eyes watered in the bright light. "What?"

"I'm not going back for Charlie," he repeated, but calmly, like ordering groceries. "With the land trackless like this, it might take a week to find him. And, hey, I'm tied to my work."

I stared at the big man. I listened for malice toward Charlie but detected none. I felt that clenching in my bowels and stomach that signaled fear: my disenchantment with Charlie was one thing, my abandoning him something else.

The detective explained that Charlie remained four hours indeterminably northeast in the Tenere region. He'd be happy to notify the police in Zinder, who would send a patrol searching for him. These police were experts, constantly combing the area for stranded French tourists and that I shouldn't worry. In turn, the big man recommended that I continue with him to Lome. I'd work for him, searching for Raymont and his girlfriend in the couple of weeks it would take for Charlie to hitch his way south.

It was difficult and inconvenient for the detective to retrace our route to Charlie, I agreed. I also recognized that I had the option of remaining behind in Tanout and mounting my own search. But Tanout was sandy and desolate. The sun burned on the back of my neck. It made me realize how much I didn't want to spend another night on a foam mattress in a filthy, mosquito-ridden room. Then again, I had no money. How would I hire a car and guide to mount my search? I'd have to do it alone. Mr. Fitzwater began sounding sensible. In Lome, at least I had a way to make money and could plan to meet up with my dad. Thus I judged the choice of making my way alone back to Charlie through hundreds of miles of Sahel an absurd one compared to riding comfortably to Lome with the black man. Thus I rationalized that accepting a ride from Mr. Fitzwater now meant a better chance of finding my father later. And still my frustration with Charlie coupled with my fear of being stranded in Tanout also influenced my decision—how could they not? I didn't want to be left in the kicked-up dust of the departing Volare, like Charlie had. I didn't want to spend another night alone near that proprietor with the tire treads on his cheeks.

"Wait, Harlon, I'm coming!" I burst out, and trotted around the car and jumped into Charlie's seat.

"Very good, Murray," Mr. Fitzwater said in his rich deep voice, moving behind the steering wheel. "Pleased to have the company."

The detective looked huge and black in his rusting convertible. The car smelled like pine from its cardboard tree air freshener. I snapped my fingers nervously to the reggae music's beat as the big man drove us out of Tanout. By evening, Charlie would know we weren't coming back for him. He'd pace his patch of sand in the dying sun, wavy gray hair blowing about in the cooling breeze, and guess my cowardice. He'd understand, chubby white hands gripped behind his back, that hell could be a sun-heated American car and Satan a charming black man with the best of tales.

PART III

The Mission

SIX

1

Escape from Charlie proved heady, an intoxicating freedom that I'd never before felt. I belted out reggae songs, laughed uproariously at the detective's jokes as we drove south. (Mr. Fitzwater kept forestalling my guilt with, "Charlie's all right, Muz.") It made my last somber month with Charlie seem like a bad memory. It invested my new world, a world no longer subject to Charlie's moral censure, with a deep fascination: from stick-thin Muslims in toe-length pastel robes and white lace skullcaps in northern Niger, to bare-breasted market women and gaff-rigged house boats in Niamey, to the hundred rust shades of the cracked land past Ougadougou, the wild boars and antelope of the savannah, the rainforest halfway down Togo's spine, coastal Lome (rhymes with olé), its casinos, palm trees, boulevards, luxury hotels, its fishing dories that netted grouper in the green-blue Bight de Benin.

Escape from Charlie. I learned to appreciate the world sensually; I was provoked to cast off quickly Judaism's ritual yoke: first I stopped praying, then eating kosher, then Sabbath observance. This would have happened sooner or later even in Israel—would it not?—especially in light of my shocking perception in Algiers that my years of Talmud learning hadn't been morally internalized one jot. Nevertheless, I sought reasons for this casting-off phenomenon, how Orthodox observance could be brushed away like so much lint after only two weeks.

I found my answer in Lome. The detective was navigating

the capital's rotaries and sandy streets at sundown on our arrival, the second week in December 1980, driving us past town center with its fruit and fish smells and salt breezes from the sea, past the tables and lemon yellow Spam can lights of women street food vendors and the whiter electric lights of the steel and glass luxury hotels towering over the palms that ran along the capital's stretch of beach. I was already nonobservant, not yet worried about confronting Charlie in two weeks: he was out of sight and so out of influence. My deceptively simple and breathtakingly wrong answer came in two parts. I rationalized, part one, that Judaism had always been *Charlie's* life—I'd been coerced into it all along. And, part two, if I couldn't do *all* the mitzvoth properly due to my lack of belief, then I'd do none of them at all because I refused to be a hypocrite. Which, of course, was baloney. I just didn't want, as Vivian would say, cognitive dissonance. I didn't want the discomfort of contradictions that would be too evidently present if I observed one mitzvah and not another. Instead, I sought mental comfort in Mr. Fitzwater's food, drink, and his stupid job, a type of Valium oblivion to stay my ever-encroaching guilt about leaving Charlie, stay my intellectual dishonesty about forsaking my religion.

This clarity in my motives occurred only months later. At the time the detective and I arrived in Lome, I was merely eager for experience. I wanted to taste the world, somehow make its beauty and decrepitude my own, have stories to tell, like my mentor. I say, "mentor," because I let the detective be just that. I let him buy me knee-length Bermuda shorts and a Hawaiian shirt with bright purple macaws to replace my desert-tattered Orthodox suit, and listened eagerly to his stories and advice how to search out Raymont: check the tourist hotels on a staggered but frequent schedule, check the beaches, restaurants, and fancy clothes boutiques, the wealthier residential quarters, Catholic churches, outdoor food markets. Make friends with the working people: bartenders, policemen, shopkeepers, market ladies, waiters, desk clerks, and kids everywhere. Learn French. Buy everyone Cokes. Smile lots and tell jokes. If Raymont showed up, I'd find out.

That first evening in Lome, the detective parked Lena near the beach shack of a large hotel, the Hotel de Golfe. I followed him around a gravel path to the beach hut's front. White people drank on a cement patio; waves crashed across a darkened beach. We stepped inside the thatch-roofed shack where Mr. Fitzwater introduced me to a short energetic man and a pair of middle-aged waitresses tending a scratched mahogany bar. *"Monsieur Napolean, Carmel et Ruth, voici Murray Orloff!"* He flourished his arm at me like I was a prize on a game show. I smiled and bobbed my head. The Africans gazed back stonily, their eyeballs orange under the shack's low-wattage bulbs.

The detective kept talking French. Napolean and the waitresses started nodding. Soon the waitress named Ruth was leading the detective and me from the shack and walking us down the beach road a half mile east to her family's walled-in house, called a "consession," where I was shown to a square cement room containing nothing but a bed and broken dresser.

Mr. Fitzwater spent the night at the Hotel de Golfe. The following morning, he drove me around town and showed me the odd places Raymont might turn up: hole-in-the wall cafés, a billiards hall run by a Lebanese midget with cataracts, named Foyt, a voodoo and fetish market, a seedy bar for Gauloise-smoking French tourists. By noon, we were back at Ruth's. The detective gave me food money and money to stand people drinks. He wished me luck. He told me that he'd be back in a few weeks, then drove away.

The following day and mornings after that, I hiked around Lome. The sun reddened my cheeks and forearms. I lost weight. At lunchtime, I smoked cigarettes and napped in the air-conditioned lobbies of luxury hotels. By early afternoon, I began my rounds to the stores, markets, and residential quarters, to the American Embassy where I posted a sign for Charlie telling him my address. Occasionally, I hiked through Lome's shantytown or sat at white-people bars, reading *The Herald Tribune* or scribbling impressionistic postcards to Mother, Louise, and Max. I never mentioned, of course, that Charlie was gone.

At dusk, I taxied to Napolean's beach shack to swim. I'd change my clothes, wade into the Bight, and crawl past the breakers into the peaks and valleys of waves. I turned on my back and floated; I flopped to my belly and stretched my cupped hands forward in the cool green water, crawling east toward a disused pier. Near its barnacled moorings, I grasped the ladder's slimy rung, waves and undertows coursing strongly about me. I greeted the old men who fished there, then swam back upbeach. I dressed. Ruth served me beer. I walked to town for street food—goat meat with tomato sauce, rice, gumbo, chicken brochettes—then began my night rounds.

Three months passed. Days of hot salty humidity, languid afternoons, and spicy food, calypso music in the bars at night. Crescendos of anticipation to find Raymont, crescendos of fear and hope that Charlie might appear.

I say, "hope," because the glamor of my freedom from Charlie and religion started fading. My routine after a month bored me and I grew lonely for my family and friends. Physical pleasures like treif food, swimming, and cigarettes became no big deal. (I don't list sex because I hadn't yet, or ever, slept with a woman; I was too poor to court a white one and African women didn't attract me.)

Then coup d'état bombs began exploding in Lome and my eden of illicit delights crumbled before my eyes. Squads of soldiers patrolled the streets and beat up civilians. Mr. Fitzwater, frustrated with the search for Raymont, turned hostile toward me.

This happened at the end of my third month in Lome, after I knew that Charlie wasn't going to show up: he was either staying at Daniel's or, failing a rapprochement, had traveled home. In the meantime, I'd had news of my uncle. A British missionary come to Lome for supplies described "Danny" to me as "a tall, humpbacked chap who likes cigars." Until then, I had no desire to look him up—I might run into my dad and I wasn't ready for that. But since there was no longer any good reason to remain in Lome, I asked Mr. Fitzwater to make it worth my while. The terms were an airplane ticket to Israel at the end of the search, successful or not.

The detective scoffed, "Do I look like your daddy, Muz?" He sat in a wicker chair at the far end of Ruth's second-story porch. He was fresh from the casinos and dressed in a brown pinstripe suit and yellow silk tie. He fingered his cufflinks and patted his hair slicked with Afrosheen, which smelled like vanilla extract.

"Then lend me the money for the ticket," I asked.

"You're joking me, yeah?"

"But all this is your fault!" I meant that he seduced me to come to Lome at the expense of my father.

"No way, babe!" the big man snapped back. "You could have refused to come with me in Tanout. You could have left me any time after that. Hell, you can go this instant if you want." And he gestured toward the screen door.

"But there was nothing in Tanout. I had to come with you."

The detective jeered, "Doesn't the great Jew God take care of his own?"

"That's your fault," I said. "I don't believe in that stuff anymore."

The detective sprung out of his chair. He grabbed my shirt. "*None* of your troubles is my fault, boy! You're just too scared to go it alone. Ha, you're so damn worried about your own ass that you can't even decide if you need to take a crap!" He shoved me backward. My head bounced off the mosquito screening. "Two weeks. That's all you got, man," he warned me. "Then I give up on you like you gave up on your old man." He whipped open the porch door and stamped down the stairs. The aluminum compound door rattled until he reached the street.

I slouched against the porch screening. Ruth emerged from the apartment's insides. She sat in her wicker rocker and patted the stool next to her for me to come and sit. She lit a pipe and rocked as she puffed. I leaned away from the screening and slid onto the stool, noticing how her black-gray hair pompadoured off her forehead and how her profile in the dark smoky air resembled an African tribal mask, bloated in line and feature, almost demonic. But I was dazed at the rough true things Mr. Fitzwater had said to me. Ruth reached out her hand and held mine, sensing this. Her fingers were dry and calloused and she squeezed and loosened them around mine, pulselike. A long time seemed to pass. Finally, matter-of-factly, she said, "Fitzwater's going to throw you away like dog scraps, Murray, and he's going to throw you away next time."

"So you heard him talk to me." I watched Lome's lights flicker in the middle distance and listened to the fire engines whine from town center. Another "freedom" bomb had exploded. Patcha Kulibaba, leader of the revolutionary National Congress, was escalating his guerrilla war against President Gnassingbe Eyadema. The capital now seemed to be continually aflame, alive with ambulances and streams of water aimed into smoking buildings, people saving possessions from ruins, roadblocks, squads of soldiers beating people, lines of taxis driving people out of town, the wild-eyed shouting of President Eyadema on national TV.

"How are you going to live when Fitzwater tells you to go?" Ruth asked, reminding me of the fate of penniless white men in Africa. "What are you going to eat?"

Her question scared me since I saw these ex-administrators from embassies and foreign aid programs every day. They'd been fired for drunkenness and now were dressed in ragged clothes and slept in the doorways of buildings. They worked petty jobs for beer and cigarettes.

"Don't know," I mumbled. Fear cramped my stomach. I found myself squeezing her hand.

Ruth waited for me to become sufficiently alarmed. She then proposed I deliver, for a hefty fee, a belt of coup d'etat money to an agent of Kulibaba's past the roadblocks that sealed off Lome. I sighed. Who could be surprised that Ruth worked for Kulibaba? Who knew who anyone was anymore? I listened to her arguments that I was suited for the task: I was a white man, I knew Lome, the gendarmes knew me.

Ruth's offer was storybook dangerous but tempting. Mr. Fitzwater's hostility had shattered my naïveté that he cared about me at all. Soon, he'd strand me poor in Lome. Indeed, he'd leave me with fewer qualms than when I walked away from Charlie. My skin, nevertheless, pricked with sweat when I accepted Ruth's offer. I sweated more a week later when a slim, toffee-hued man named Twilly parked his blue Peugeot in front of Ruth's compound. "That's him, Murray." Ruth instructed me that Twilly would drive me on the courier job, that I was to tell the gendarmes I was traveling to Kpalime to visit a girlfriend. Twilly strapped a thick money belt to my abdomen, like a fetal monitor.

And soon, far too soon, Twilly and I were motoring down Rue de Tivoli to Rue de Quinze Fevrier, the hard-topped loop circling Lome, passing sandy streets of residential houses and colonial mansions with their high protective walls, passing leaching fields stinking with sewage and Lome's shantytown, which provided Kulibaba with so many of his recruits. And soon, too soon, we were inching forward in the line of cars to the roadblock and then it was our turn. The gendarmes—I knew none of them—surrounded the car. They examined Twilly's papers, opened the Peugeot's trunk. I mentioned my girl in Kpalime; the gendarmes laughed. They waved us forward. It was that easy.

I pounded Twilly's shoulders after we drove on. "We did it, Twilly!"

"Yes, sah." Twilly mopped his brow with a handkerchief.

I lit cigarettes for both of us. I saw the Kpalime road run straight and west into the rainforest. Trees and undergrowth were a bright green from the new rains. Bush taxis and troop carriers passed us going the other way, toward Lome. I spotted crows when we turned off the paved road just south of Kpalime, and antelope, wild boar, tethered goats in a village whose mud walls were topped with shards of glass to keep out thieves, naked children, baobab branches strung with fetish dolls, farmers dressed in calf-length robes, women crouched under giant head sacks of charcoal, a rabid dog. The air held an odor of mildew. Trees blocked the sun. Distantly, I heard chain saws.

The muddy road sloped downward, traversing a culvert bridge, climbing to a second village of wood bungalows. Twilly parked the Peugeot beside a Land Rover. He led me onto the patio of a wood building, a patio crowded with men, plants, and animal cages containing hamsters, mice, weasels, and bush rats. A faded, damp-rotted sign in English read, "The Jungle Bar."

Inside, stood potted palms, bird cages housing African grays, marsh owls, thrushes, and sunbirds. Crocodiles lay inert in a long cement tub, which ran along one wall. The big brown inert animals were draped over each other like thick slices of tongue. Men dressed in long pants and long-sleeved shirts, muddy from forest work, sat at round tables. A barman scraped foam from mugs of draught beer with a tongue depressor while a ceiling fan knifed slowly through the ammoniac stink of the animal waste.

Twilly led me past a bead curtain, through a back room. Three women sat on low stools and hammered meat. He led me out the rear doorway, back outside. I followed him up a dirt path to a dilapidated bungalow. A voodoo face was carved into its door panel. Twilly once more became nervous as he knocked.

The door opened a crack. A white man, shadows obscuring his face, peeked out. Recognizing Twilly, he let the door swing open. Twilly and I followed the man into his bungalow, into a spacious living room lit by a lone kerosene lantern. The furnishings of the room—the bamboo table and chairs, the antelope head mounted on the wall, the collection of tribal masks—donned halos in the poor light.

The white man turned and faced us. He asked us in accented French to sit down. I instantly recognized the venous complexion, the thinning silver hair, the blue eyes of Winston Raymont. Astounded, I eased myself into a bamboo chair. Twilly stood frozen in a corner of the room.

"Do you speak English or French better, young man?" he asked me.

"English."

"An American," he observed, his British accent too civilized for this rainforest. "And what are you doing in Africa? The Peace Corps?" He pronounced "Corps" like corpse. He paced the room as Charlie might have, arms folded in back of him. He wore a black bathrobe with white buttons up its front, like a woman's housecoat.

"I'm looking for my lost uncle." I wondered if Raymont knew that I worked for Harlon Fitzwater.

"And I suppose this uncle got lost on his way to market." Raymont chuckled, a short owlish hoot that made his silver hair quiver.

"I'm telling you the truth," I lied.

"I'm sure you are, young man. Quite sure. But there are no white men in Africa who aren't running away from something. Yes?"

I nodded, admitted his point.

"But you have the money, of course."

I patted my abdomen.

"Please give us a look."

I shimmied the money belt out of my Bermuda shorts. Raymont sat near me at the bamboo table, counting the bills. "It's all here," he finally said, and smiled. "Good work. Now all we need is for Kulibaba to win."

"What does it matter? Whoever wins will be horrible."

"Granted," the aging man said, "but if Kulibaba wins then I can leave this detestable rainforest."

"Why not leave now?"

"Because I am, as you Americans say, on the lam."

"You're hiding out."

"The Togolais government gave me sanctuary when no other country would," he said, "and for that I am thankful. But the cost of that sanctuary is this rainforest, and I've grown to despise the cost." He sighed painfully. He frowned at the tatters of his life. After a moment, his despair seemed to energize him and he strode over to me. "You're absolutely right that I don't give a good goddamn what these Africans do to themselves. But since I made a ghastly mistake because of a woman who has since left me, I must now extricate myself from that mistake."

Raymont fussed with the kerosene lamp. Light spurted up around him and glowed around the edges of his black robe, like an eclipse. The halos about the bamboo furniture vanished and he stepped toward me again. He gripped the arms of my chair, leaning forward so that he towered over me.

"I needed sanctuary, young man," he repeated, paste-white face almost touching mine. "But now all I want is a stroll in the sun. This rainforest depresses me." He stared into my lap, voice cracking. "I wish to God I hadn't killed those people." He closed his eyes. He collected himself and lifted his head. "Look, I know your name is Orloff and that you've been looking for me." His voice hardened. He watched me with his yellow malarial eyes. "Just know that you won't be able to touch me as long as I stay in the forest." He said this I think more to reassure himself than to put me off. "But don't worry about eventually getting me, Orloff. No one gives a damn, nor should they, about decrepit old men who kill people. Somebody from the revolution will inform on me to the government." He frowned at his prophecy. "Because, you understand, Kulibaba will not succeed. The French will prop up Eyadema like they propped up Mobutu in Zaire. Somebody will then want to save his own skin, and when it's known that I've bitten the hand that's fed me, President Eyadema will hand me over to the government of Niger who will prosecute me and have me shot. Pow, pow." Raymont snapped his fingers, like gunshots. "And to think I allowed that slut Babette to talk me into blowing up that reactor." Raymont slicked back his silver hair and inhaled deeply, like he was exercising. "But it was I who set the detonators, wasn't it, my dear Orloff? And just as it was my mistake so now it's my tough luck. Ha," he hooted bitterly, "how we all of us yearn to do the right thing and we . . . we . . . kill people." He released the arms of my bamboo chair and stepped backward into the room's center. He stood in the black robe in the poor yellow light of the kerosene lamp, his face twisted with pain.

And as I was able that moment to feel the man's horror of what he'd done, a horror of waste and irrevocability, like a teenager dying in a car accident, so did he in his black housecoat and dilapidated bungalow seem the embodiment of the dark recesses of my own soul. And forced to peer at what I might resemble in forty years, I jumped quickly from my chair and motioned to Twilly that it was time to go. I said to the aging drunk, "May God have pity upon us both," and followed Twilly down the shadowy hall of the bungalow, back into the rainforest. Calypso music and electric lights beckoned to us from The Jungle Bar. The moonless night was black beneath the crown of trees.

2

Twilly raced the blue Peugeot back toward Lome, bugs splattering against the windshield. Trees and dense shrubbery along the road were high black walls. The night was clear with stars, moonless. We smoked cigarettes and listened to music. The vent sprayed out asphalt-stinking air.

After an hour, we sighted the line of cars waiting to enter Lome. The road was curved and lined with trees, banked above the undergrowth that crowded its sides. We crawled along with the line of cars, toward the gendarmes' checkpoint. We drove close enough to view the guard booth and its turnstile, a pair of gendarmes squatting by a brush fire.

I left the car to relieve myself. I stepped past the row of trees and slid down the steep road bank into the undergrowth. I climbed back up and saw our Peugeot had reached the guard booth. I ran to catch up but stopped when I saw a gendarme peer closely at Twilly's papers. I moved to the side of the road when the gendarme called over his friends. In the darkness of the trees, I watched Twilly's papers examined a second and third time. Raymont's crossed us, I thought. A big gendarme slammed Twilly against the Peugeot then. A second gendarme punched his face.

I slid once more down the embankment into the lightless undergrowth. I hunched down and traced the curve of road, toward Lome—I wanted my six hundred dollars courier fee. Thorns scratched me in the dark trench. Cars raced by along the road above.

I hiked in the trench a long time. When I climbed back up to look around, the guard booth was gone. Miles ahead of me, Lome's skyline glimmered with electric lights, with the fires from Kulibaba's bombs.

I walked the road in the moonless night. I reached Lome's

shantytown and veered off into the leaching fields when I saw army Jeeps. I crossed the acres of grass and human waste and stepped onto Rue de Quinze Fevrier. Stars dimmed under the streetlights' glare.

Lome seemed like a sheet of flame—this might be Kulibaba's final coup d'état push. The wide boulevard was crowded with people on foot and in taxis. Trucks were piled high with luggage and mattresses. Everyone streamed north, out of town.

I hiked the boulevard to unpaved sandy Rue de Tivoli and heard the sea. The humid air smelled like fish. My quarter's electricity was severed, the corner bar padlocked. Houses with their protective walls loomed above me, miniature castles in the night.

I pushed past the splintered door to Ruth's compound. The courtyard was spooky feeling without wives or kids. I climbed the stairs to the second-story landing and strode onto the darkened porch, calling, "Ruth, I'm back!" I checked the house for her but she was gone. "Damn you, Ruth!" I walked back to the porch, Lome blazing beyond the mosquito screening.

"Looking for these, Muz?" Mr. Fitzwater's voice was familiar, deep.

I looked left: the big man sitting in Ruth's wicker rocker at the far end of the porch was holding up a fist of dollars. Dull red light from the bomb fires washed over his face and made his teeth bright. He wore a suit and tie and smelled like vanilla extract.

"Where's Ruth?"

"She's gone, son." The detective faced burning Lome. "You got any information for me, Muz?" And he rubbed his fingers together so the money made noise.

I pictured Winston Raymont in his woman's housecoat in his rainforest bungalow, his pasty-white face creased with pain.

"You know where he is, don't you?" The big man lowered his fist of bills.

"Yes." Why'd I say that?

"But you're not going to tell me, are you?"

"No, I don't think so." I surprised myself because I certainly felt no obligation to protect Raymont, especially since I believe he crossed me. I was just tired of being cowed by Mr. Fitzwater, tired of my cowardice in abandoning Charlie and Judaism, tired, really, of being a punk. And though I was certain I could swap Raymont's whereabouts for my money and buy that plane ticket home, I didn't want to abandon Charlie a second time.

"Where's Raymont?" The big man leaned forward in the wicker rocker. He tapped his fingernails against an arm of the chair and held up the money in his other hand.

I stared at the bills and shrugged, only growing more disgusted at my chronic self-pity.

"All right." The detective's voice remained calm. "You tell me where the man is and I give back your money *and* buy you a plane ticket home." His fingernails drummed the rocker's arm. He waited huge and black in the chair.

"I can't do that," I said, but quietly. The shameful memory of the morning in Tanout when I blurted out, "Wait, I'll come with you!" kept me now from selling out Raymont and therefore Charlie for the ticket.

"What do you mean you can't?" The detective stood from his rocker, amazed.

"I can't do that," I repeated, too nervous to say anything else. I backed away from him.

"Last chance for that plane ticket, Muz."

My back struck a joist of the porch. "No thanks."

"I see we need to have a heart-to-heart talk." And he sprang to grab me.

I rushed past the screen door as his hand grazed my collar and took the stairs three at a time. I ran through the dark, empty courtyard, past the splintered door of Ruth's compound, to sandy Rue de Tivoli.

The detective caught up with me on Rue de Quinze Fevrier. He grabbed my Hawaiian shirt and jerked me close. "Where's Raymont?" His breath was hot and wet in my face. He clenched the back of my neck and marched me away from the stream of people who hiked out of town. He was steering me back onto Rue de Tivoli when his foot snagged in the sand.

I jerked free from him. I pushed back through the people to the empty side of the boulevard. I sprinted past the line of cars to the corridor of palms that bordered the beach. I figured I might lose him in the trees, but he closed on me.

I raced to the gray-black waterline, sucking air into my cigarette-rotten lungs, like an asthmatic, and turned upbeach. Ahead of me stood the disused pier and the beach hut. The big man swiped at me beneath the piles. I veered right and climbed onto the lip of the dock. I raced down the staggered beams to the pier's end, noting the tide moved seaward. The undertow would be too strong to risk swimming now. Behind me, the big man hovered yards away. His arms were spread wide so that I couldn't slip by. "A plane ticket for Raymont," he offered once more, breathless from our run.

I panted, too. Small waves lapped the pier's thick moorings; water hissed from barnacles. My fear of the black man was keen. But the shame of facing my mother after abandoning Charlie twice weighed heavier upon me still and I shook my head.

"You're a fool to get yourself hurt for an old man you don't even know, Murray, a man who kills people," the big man said, and inched closer to me, his arms opened wide, like he held a medicine ball.

I glanced at the splintery beams of the pier to make sure of my footing, at the open spaces between its slats and winch spikes that resembled small spears. I looked at the detective who circled in on me and I almost told him about Raymont until I realized that my fear of the big man had turned to anger, like when Charlie bullied me. "You know, it isn't Raymont at all, Harlon," I said, my voice steady now. "It's just that I'm so tired of you."

And I charged the big man to surprise him, but he tripped me to the pier. He yanked me to my knees and punched me hard in the nose. Searing pain shot through my temples. I tasted blood. I lurched forward and grabbed his thighs, like a tired boxer. The big man circled my waist with his arms and lifted me high. He moved his hands around to my belly to slam me back onto the dock. But I held on to his hair as he threw me, and he lost his balance. His leg slipped into an open space between the beams. The big man began to sink even as he held me high. His body jolted to a stop as his hip reached the pier. My weight pitched his face forward and down onto a winch spike, and I fell off into the sea.

The salt water stung my nose where the detective hit me. The tide dragged me away from shore. I crawled some strokes to the slimy ladder and hoisted myself up to the dock. My wet clothes felt heavy as sand. The black man lay prone, head to knees, like a dancer who stretched her legs. He still breathed.

Sirens and shouts came back into my hearing. I noticed the fires in the luxury hotels, the red enflamed branches of burning palms. I kicked the detective hard in his ribs to make sure that he was knocked out good and then rifled his pockets for my money. I folded the bills into my underwear and waited on the pier's end for the tide to turn, until the waves pulsed in long and thick, like wind blowing wheat, and soldiers with flashlights emerged from the corridor of palms. Then I stripped off my shirt and pants and knotted them about my waist. I slipped into the black chilly ocean and breaststroked outward, rising and sinking in the troughs of the swells. When Lome blurred to a scrim of flame, I turned west for the mile swim to Ghana. I swam arm over arm and floated on my back when I grew tired. My bruised nose healed in the bite of the salt.

SEVEN

The tide carried me past Lome's fires and lights, the whine of police vans and fire engines, until the coast darkened, resembling a thin curved lip. I knew that I'd reached Ghana but swam farther to make sure, always breaststroking outside the breakers' edge.

I headed for shore finally. There was a rush with the breakers, a tumble in the black foam. I paused, on all fours, to catch my breath on the wet sand, then stumbled up the beach into the border of palms. I wrung out my clothes and put them on. I lay down on the dry, still-warm sand, closed my eyes, and fell asleep.

The gulls woke me after sunrise. The dirty-white birds hovered beyond the breakers and screeched for fish. Itchy from the sand, I rinsed off in the ocean and spread my clothes on some roots to dry. I shivered naked in the corridor of palms. My arms were achy from my swim, my nose tender from the detective's fist.

I dressed and waded through a band of dense shrubbery to the cracked-up coastal road to Accra, Ghana's capital. I'd decided once more to buy an Israel plane ticket. Charlie would already be back in Jerusalem or he wouldn't: I was too drained to care anymore what Mother might say. I'd overcome my cowardice by standing up to Mr. Fitzwater, and this seemed good enough for the time being, a major accomplishment. Yet as my stomach cramped with hunger and I grew tired walking this road which curved then straightened then curved, an anxious feeling washed over me that I couldn't pin down, like a dream of endless rooms where one long hall ends at a door that opens into another long hall. It was an anxiety I couldn't dismiss, that plagued me as I tramped along in the sun and humidity and finally perched myself on a tree stump to wait for a car, that belied my sense of having faced something major and courageously passed.

Late afternoon. The sun orange-red. Gnats swarmed near my eyes. A motorcycle buzzed into sight, from the direction of Lome. I waved my arms and the driver slowed. A Peace Corps Volunteer also fleeing the coup, a thirty-year-old self-professed semialcoholic named James Winner. "The only time I have a drinking problem is when I can't find a drink," he said. James wore green work pants and a sleeveless white T-shirt. He lent me his spare motorcycle helmet and kicked down the bike's back footpegs so I could climb up.

The savannah blurred to a sheet of green as we took off. My eyes teared in the wind. James and I shouted our coup stories to each other. He was acne-scarred, scruffy bearded. He told me about coal miners in Wilkes-Barre and bought me gourds of palm wine in Keta, Cape St. Paul, Ada, and Tema. The alcoholic buzz felt good after the stress of Lome, and I missed Mother, Louise, and Max, my yeshiva friends. The fact that I wasn't religious anymore nor planned to be didn't bother my sentimentality: I just wanted to go home.

In Accra, James drove me to the Air Ghana office, a suite of rooms in a brick building constructed by the English in colonial times. The ticketing agents were slim men and ebony women dressed in blue and green suits. The air-conditioning felt wonderful after Accra's heat. When a woman attendant asked to help me, James moved over to the office's smoky windows, nearer the vents. He stared outside into the market of tailors and letter writers, at the bush women squatting over their bundles of sticks and hustlers selling their watches and cigarettes. I leaned against the Formica counter and explained to the woman that I wanted a ticket to Israel and would six hundred dollars take me that far?

The pretty woman—polished nails, teased-out hair, the tan complexion that showed me she was half white—punched my facts into her computer. Five hundred dollars would be all it took to get me to Tel Aviv via Rome, she said. In fact, there was a plane to Rome and connecting flight to Israel this evening. Would I care to reserve?

"Yes." I fingered the still damp bills and my damp passport in my pocket as the woman wrote up the ticket. Jerusalem felt real that second—family, friends, the Wailing Wall— and energy coursed through me, like caffeine.

"I hope you had a restful stay with us in Ghana, sah," she chatted.

"Terrific. Gorgeous country," I said, glancing at James and past the office's windows, at the young men in pink sunglasses and tight pants, who hawked cheap radios and watches, at the ragged cripples who begged passersby for change. These cripples killed my excitement, though. They reminded me of Charlie who might be at Daniel's this second and hurt or penniless, who was now counting on me to show up.

"You have been staying with us in Ghana a long time, sah?" The woman stamped and initialed my ticket's sheets.

"I swam over from Lome last night," I joked, trying to resuscitate my excitement about going home. But I remembered my whole swim came about because I wished to recapture some moral integrity and I wondered seriously for the first time if I shouldn't go to Daniel's mission instead of Israel.

"Sign on this X and this X, sah." The woman tapped her red fingernails to the proper places on the ticket.

I borrowed her pen and signed the X's, feeling guilty. My previous bravado that I didn't care what Mother might say when I showed up nonreligious and without her husband withered. Such unconcern struck me now more as a function of palm wine than reality. I mean, how in the world would I explain these things to her?

The woman retrieved the ticket from me. She tore and sorted its parts, asking, "How do you wish to pay, sah?"

I managed to say, "Cash," as I gripped my damp bills and stared at her, imagining myself in the Air Ghana plane as it lifted off from the runway that night: the plane's blue and green metal skin, the beige cabin and yellow land lights below, the stewardesses who would serve me one of those lousy meals. . . .

"Sah," she was saying to me and holding out her hand. "It is the time to pay."

I actually extended my arm to give the woman the money but at the last second drew back, understanding finally what my anxiety had been on the road to Accra before James picked me up, what had trailed me all this way: my subconscious conviction that a decision to return to Israel was the same type of cowardly decision as abandoning Charlie in Tanout. True bravery wasn't only fighting Harlon Fitzwater, I realized unhappily, but was also, and perhaps more so, the courage to travel to Daniel's mission and confront my dad despite what he'd say about my abandoning him and how he'd rant when I showed up nonreligious and insisted on staying so. And still my realization might not have stopped me from purchasing the ticket except that last night in Lome I'd said no to Mr. Fitzwater when I'd so wanted to say yes. I'd stopped my cycle of irresponsibility, however obliquely, when I refused his reward. And as my refusal took guts—the big man could really have hurt me—it became valuable to me, a piece of moral coinage not to blow and whose only way of not being squandered was to travel north and face Charlie. So I lowered my fist with the bills in it; I backed away from the ticket counter, mumbling something dumb. The pretty attendant scowled at me as I strode out of the office, back into the heat and noise of dirty Accra.

And though I knew that I'd made the correct decision— my anxiety melted away as I climbed up behind James on the Yamaha and as we motored slowly past the crowds and tethered animals of the market, finding the road north out of Accra—my underlying and ever-present fear of Charlie resurfaced, a dull throbbing ache compared to my keen physical fear of the detective, and yet one that struck deeper chords within me. My fear of the detective remained solely physical while my fear of Charlie was based on discord running through my entire life. It was a discord that had attained epic proportions in my mind, like the impending death of a loved one, and badly needed resolution.

But the most important thing, I reminded myself, was that I'd decided to confront Charlie, to inform him that I refused to bend to his will any longer. Which gave me, on paper, a comfortable sense of doing the right thing. But which also locked me right back into a fear of my father that grew and grew as James and I traveled farther north, over coastal flats, tindery hills, and steep jungle peaks, cliffs with misty views and villages of paillotes denuded from the first storms of the rainy season. We rode through forests of cottonwood and sapele trees, past Kumasi, Mampong, Ejura, and Atebubu, with James pausing innumerable times for drinks. Then we took a ferry across the Volta River, and motored through Salaga, Tamale, and the savannah, to the town of Madugari, where I hugged James goodbye and began the twenty-mile walk to Dapongo along a dirt road muddy from the new rains and that wound through cassava fields and twisted down from a plateau.

I trudged along, my fear of Charlie always with me, like a birthmark, the sun a yellow smudge behind dark clouds. I wondered if Daniel would recognize me after all these years and if Charlie's reappearance at the mission had been salt to his unhealed wounds. Maybe, after all, theirs had been a good reunion. It was a curiosity that kept me walking all day, through yam fields and across charred acres of slash-and-burn agriculture, until I reached the Mono River at dusk, a cocoa-colored torrent washing whole trees by me. An ancient British tugboat ferried me to the Togo shore. I bribed the douaniers to let me enter the country with my expired visa. The officers told me, divvying up my fifty bucks, that Daniel's Baptist mission lay fourteen more kilometers down the road. But it was too late to hike there today, and I climbed the steep dirt road after the river, looking for a place to sleep in the approaching dark.

I found a leafy baobab tree and sat beneath it, feeling rain. I chewed bread bought in Madugari and sucked mangoes I'd collected along the way. I watched the line of sky and land blur in the rain and night and spun out my curiosity about Charlie and Daniel. I imagined the brothers greeting each other beneath an eave of a Baptist mission thatch hut. The one brother was short and fat, the older brother tall but humpbacked. Naked children chased guinea fowl around a smoke-filled yard. A toothless grandmother stirred a pot of millet gruel.

"Well, if it isn't Chuck Orloff!" Daniel said cheerfully, a half-smoked stogie cocked in the corner of his mouth. "How the hell have your years been, brother?"

"Not bad by all accounts," Charlie answered, dusty and tan from the Sahara, "but I missed you, Danny. How I missed you."

"I missed you, too, Chuck," Daniel said, embarrassed by the emotion, thinking, I hardly know the man. But Charlie was sincere and he confessed, "I was expecting you, Chuck. I was hoping that you'd come."

"But all those years, Danny. And not even a postcard."

"You have to appreciate, Chuck, that Rachael's death just . . . just . . . blew me away." Daniel gazed off into the trees. He flicked a tear away from his eye with his cigar hand.

The brothers stood silently beneath the thatch hut's eave, Daniel with a wood crucifix circling his neck, Charlie with his black velvet yarmulke. Children ran through the smoky yard; the grandmother tasted her kettle of gruel.

"And isn't it funny how Rachael turned us both religious," Charlie observed after a time.

The dying sun colored the palms orange. Birds cawed from their fronds.

"And how we hated it as kids!" Daniel cried out, to ease the sadness.

But Charlie remained intense, his voice finally choking up. "Forgive me, Danny," he suddenly wailed. "Forgive me for everything."

Daniel smiled at Charlie, then, like a doctor with good news, news that you could never expect to hear. "I forgive you, Chuck," he said, and reached out his cigar hand to touch Charlie's shoulder. Charlie opened his own arms. The long-lost brothers would embrace beneath the heatless sun. . . .

But perhaps Charlie wouldn't be so apologetic for ancient wrongs against his brother, if any, and he'd descend into Daniel's life like a Cossack into a Sukkah. He'd despise

Daniel's Christianity and his church, an intolerance that would overwhelm any patience Charlie mustered for the occasion, that would turn their reunion into a cacophony of name-calling and accusations.

My night beneath the baobab proved a cold and wet one. I stood up feverish in the day's first gray light to finish the trek to Daniel's mission. I followed the dirt road through wheat fields and tiny villages. Eventually, I felt that odd soreness in my spine that signaled malaria. The sky was cloudless, cobalt blue. Birds skirmished in the green trees. I rested more often as the fever gripped me, moving from a stiffness in my spine to a deep muscular ache and temple-rending headache.

It was early afternoon when I reached the mission: a circle of huts screened from the road by a brake of trees. My body was by turns shivery and hot. I walked up a gravel driveway to a large crabgrass yard where a white woman doled out food from burlap CARE sacks to a line of African mothers holding infants. The woman had light brown hair barretted off to one side and wore jeans, a man's pink button-down shirt, silver-rimmed glasses that gave her a studious air. She looked about forty. She hurried out from behind the sacks when she saw me—I probably looked that bad.

"Please," she asked me in American-accented French, "may I help you?"

"I'm Murray Orloff and I'm looking for my uncle, Daniel Orloff," I said in English.

"Yes, of course," the woman said, putting a finger to her lips, like she needed to think fast. "We've been expecting you."

"Good," I said, taking her trepidation for concern. "But I think I have malaria. Do you have some place where I could lie down?"

"Surely," the woman said, relieved, like I'd changed a delicate subject. She led me across the crabgrass yard to an infirmary hut that stank of disinfectant, and directed me onto a bed, then rummaged in a medicine cabinet for quinine pills and aspirin.

"Is my father here?" I asked her, after I gulped down the

tablets and she tucked blankets around me. "His name is Charlie—"

"I know Charlie's name," the woman replied. "But he's not here any longer."

"So he went home," I figured, my mind hazy with the fever.

"Yes, he went home," the woman agreed, looking me over. "But you sleep now and let those pills get started. Daniel will come around when you wake up."

My headache forced me to close my eyes. I half-woke in the middle of the night. My fever was broken, my headache mostly gone. A tall man swayed in a rocker and stared at me. His eyes were black holes behind pince-nez. The light of a new moon cast his cheeks and nose and tall thin body deathly white.

I closed my eyes, alarmed that I was hallucinating from the malaria, and drifted back into a sweaty, nightmarish sleep. When I woke for real, hours later, it was still dark. The same tall man still sat in the rocker, though he napped. I left the bed to relieve myself and returned. He mumbled, a passionate whisper to a dream lover, "Oh, Patty!"

The man woke when I flopped down onto my bed. He jerked up his head and looked at me. He stood, stretched, and sat back down in the rocking chair. He pulled a cigar from his shirt pocket, tore off its plastic wrapper, and ignited a wooden match with his fingernail. He rolled the cigar's tip through the yellow flame. The tobacco cracked and sputtered. A cloud of blue smoke obscured his face as he puffed, lips smacking as he inhaled, like he tasted the smoke. I noticed the man's gray bangs of hair and blue eyes by the match light, his white oxford shirt, rolled-up sleeves, and tan khaki pants, his worn Docksider shoes—this man was my uncle.

"Hello, Uncle Daniel," I said weakly. "I can't believe it's you."

"In the living flesh, Muz," my uncle quipped in that hoarse voice of his. "But the real question is, how are you? Malaria's real hell."

"Better since the pills," I said, thinking that he hadn't

changed much over the years except for the crow's-feet around his eyes and that his back was more stooped.

"So you met Charlie," I said, recalling how the woman had said, "We've been expecting you."

"Ha, Charlie," my uncle barked. "Charlie's gone."

"He went back to Jerusalem? Without you?" They must have fought and Daniel kicked Charlie out of the mission. Maybe Charlie simply got fed up and traveled home.

"Ah, who ever knows where Charlie goes."

What an odd thing to say, I thought, as for the last dozen years none of us had known where *he'd* gone.

"But you saw him."

"Oh, yeah," Daniel said, like I'd cracked a joke. "But we'll talk about it."

"Okay." I was sorry and yet relieved to hear that Charlie wasn't here. I was willing now to talk about other matters first—Daniel seemed to want this anyway.

He asked me how Charlie and I found him out and how we came to live in Israel then, how we became religious—everything in the years since he disappeared. And while Charlie must have told him all this at their initial encounter, I figured Daniel wanted to hear my end of the story, too. Call it my victim's account.

He burst out with laughter and exclamations of surprise, as if this were the first time he'd heard any of it, and I guessed that Charlie, for whatever reasons, had suppressed details and whole sections of our history.

Daniel was impressed with our odyssey and Charlie's stubbornness in his religious pursuits. He said that he approved of Charlie applying his talents to Judaism rather than to Toys Galore. He merely sighed heavily and took off his pince-nez when I mentioned the Dutch traveler who accused Charlie of killing Rachael. He wiped them with a hankie and admitted, true, for years he'd felt that way. These bad feelings dissipated after he met Pastor Harold Allen and his wife Patty, the heads of the mission, after they invited him to build a church for them and stay on afterward as their handyman, after he began making a life for himself.

"And before the mission?" I immediately made the connection between my uncle's passionate dream whisper and the pastor's wife.

"There was no life, then."

"How do you mean?"

"I'm fifty-eight now, and besides for three years at the mission and seven years in CARE before that, what do I have to show for my life?"

I sat up in my infirmary bed and propped my lower back with a pillow. I understood my uncle to mean that for all his pre-African working years he had no family or possessions, nothing but bitter memories to show for it.

And he went on to describe his pre-Togo, post-Rachael life as two years of clerking jobs in hardware stores in various cities: Lubbock, Texas, and before that Fort Collins, Colorado, and before that Coxsackie, New York. A bleak life of rented rooms and lonely suppers in diners, cheap cars and cheap employers, drinks with low-class women in motel lounges, shopping at Zayre's, watching too much television, reading the *National Enquirer*, betting on horses and dogs. And, always, always, there was the memory of Rachael which seared through him and everything he did, like a hot brand, reminding him of his own mistakes and loveless marriage to Estelle, of his younger brother who forced him out of Toys Galore. It reminded him of his first hardware store job in Pittsfield, how they'd subsequently grown poor and had to take Rachael out of private school, how they watched her get involved with a bad crowd in public high school, watched her get involved with drugs and die.

"So Charlie *did* make you hike away from Rachael's funeral," I said.

"Really it started the morning of the funeral," Daniel said, stopping to relight his stogie and swaying in the rocker as he puffed. "Estelle put on her party dress for the temple service and I sat in my pajamas on the edge of our bed. Our daughter was dead and I was thinking, how could anyone think of having a ceremony about that? But I got dressed anyway and we drove to the Reform temple. The rabbi had us sit in the first pew of the sanctuary, in front of everyone, where I could smell the ladies' perfume. I mean, come on, my

little girl is dead and these ladies are wearing perfume?"
Daniel became angry in the dark infirmary. "The temple
service was like that, too—the phony rabbi saying those
phony things about my girl."

Daniel paused to breathe deeply, like he was living this
for the first time—it was my first sense that he was withholding something from me. After a while, his voice turned
deadpan as he described Rachael's funeral procession down
North Street and the line of cars with their headlights on, the
purple windshield stickers that read "Funeral." The procession drove through red lights and past onlookers, past the
reflections of the hearses in the windows of the hardware
store where he worked since resigning from Toys Galore.

"Then the hearses turn into Pittsfield Cemetery," Daniel
continued in the present tense, rocking in the pale moonlight
and puffing on his cigar, his own words taking him back
twelve years. "The access road curves past gravestones with
their wreaths and faded veteran flags. It's a cold sunny March
day. The limousines stop by Rachael's grave: a black hole and
pile of dirt to one side. The funeral parlor man opens the
limousine door for me and I start to cry. I can't get out of the
car until Estelle coaxes me out. I walk toward the casket. The
temple crowd huddles in front of the grave—the well-heeled
men in their overcoats, the women in their heels standing in
the half-frozen spring mud. The women look grimmer than
their husbands, but they look like the funeral parlor men—
professionally grim. I can tell that they think they are good
sports for coming out in the cold and that later they will tell
their husbands this.

"Your family drives up—Charlie and Vivian, you kids.
You all walk across the muddy cemetery ground. I stand to
one side of Rachael's casket. I listen to that phony rabbi
chanting his Psalms. What's funny is that I feel sorry for him.
He reminds me of a bad comedian in the Catskills.

"I grow sadder and sadder. My ability to put up with the
crap—the phony rabbi and the perfume, the bright party
dresses, and, yes, your father—is gone. I start to walk away
from the grave so I won't have to listen to the rabbi, so I won't
have to see Charlie and the rest of them anymore. I know that

I won't be able to take seeing my little girl lowered into the ground by those dumb gravediggers."

Wreaths of cigar smoke hovered in the warm, moonlit air. My uncle swayed back and forth in the creaky rocker, a shaded man wearing pince-nez in a smelly infirmary. He clenched his stogie between his teeth as he spoke. It made his words lisp and hardened his face into a sneer.

"From the cemetery, I walk into the Waconah Street Pub. I belt down straight whiskies and watch a golf match on television."

"But Charlie sent me into that bar looking for you!"

"I saw you come in and I ducked behind the counter," Daniel admitted. "Your eyes weren't used to the light and you didn't see me."

"But everything would have been so different if I'd seen you."

"Maybe, maybe not," Daniel said. "Anyway, I sit on my stool until the bar closes, making small talk with whoever's there—a taste of my future life. I find a ride home. Estelle yells at me when I walk in the door: how could I humiliate her in front of her friends?"

Daniel took the cigar out of his mouth. "Look, we never had the best of marriages, and I'm in this, ah, honest frame of mind. So I say, 'Estelle, how's about we call it quits. Whaddya say?' You see, in the great scheme of things we only stayed together because of the kid and now there's no kid. But she's so angry she agrees on the spot. I tell her I only want the car and a couple of hundred bucks cash. I am tipsy from the whisky and all I want is out of there. I say that I'll call her in a few months and tell her where to mail the divorce papers. And I walk out of the house in the middle of the night with no idea—but none—where I'm going."

Daniel stood up from the rocking chair. He stretched his arms up and out, his face a black oval above the patch of moonlight, then sat down and recrossed his spindly legs.

"I sign Estelle's divorce papers in Coxsackie—she never asked me to come back. A year later I move to Fort Collins. I move to Lubbock six months after that. I apply for a job with CARE, as a machine technician. I move to Africa. I meet

Pastor Allen and Patty and build them a church. I'm comfortable. I do what I need to do, though by nature I'm not a religious man. I haven't been back to the States, nor have I missed it, ever since."

My uncle finished his tale of woe as morning light, the color of his cigar ash, streamed through the window above my head and the screen door beyond us. He gazed at me intently then, once more gauging my health. "Now you'll want to hear about Charlie," he said.

His tone alarmed me. I noted a tomato stain on his oxford shirt and his eyes, which remained dark circles behind his pince-nez. I watched his bony fingers drumming his knees. I nodded, more a reflex than a display of my will, as if my body also needed to declare its readiness to hear his news.

Daniel then stood from the rocker and motioned me to follow him. He walked out of the infirmary into the cloudy morning and turned right on the crabgrass yard, hiking past the circle of huts to a thin dirt path. His curved back bent his chest toward the ground, like he was retrieving a dime. There were small nail rips in the seat of his pants.

My heart raced as I followed him past clumps of prickle bushes and grass plants with black thorns. The horrible breathlessness of his voice, "Now you'll want to hear about Charlie," cut into me like a kidney punch, as we skirted a clearing with a large shed and steel crucifix guyed to its roof—Daniel's church.

The dirt path wound through a grove of iroko trees and ended at a fenced-off plot of white crucifixes. The mission cemetery. I heard myself groaning involuntarily, "Oh, my God." Daniel opened the gate of the whitewashed fence and I followed him over the clipped lawn and past grassy mounds and dried bouquets to a far corner of the graveyard, by the freshest plot, a semiflattened mound of clotted dirt and sparse grass. My uncle's hands were folded in front of him; his gray hair fluttered in the light wind. It was how I remembered him best: standing in the Pittsfield Cemetery, grief creasing his face. I read the inscription lathed onto the crossarm of the crucifix then:

CHARLES ORLOFF 1926–1981 BELOVED BROTHER R.I.P.

"What happened?" I heard all the shock and horrible pain in my voice.

"Charlie had a heart attack four months ago."

"But he was a young man!" I cried.

Daniel shrugged his shoulders. "That's what the police said who brought his body here."

"Police? What police?" Adrenaline pumped through me. I could hardly breathe.

"The police from Niger." Daniel's voice was breathless no longer. "Charlie died where you parked him, Muz. The Niger police told me that you left him to buy a spare tire."

I panted from the adrenaline. I tried swallowing but couldn't. I imagined the parched earth and blue sky of the Sahel, the crushing pain that must have shot through my father's left arm and chest and then his alarm, his realization that this was his dismal end, his cursing me to hell with his dying breath—all these things.

My uncle said, "I'm sorry, Muz. I'm sorry for the both of us."

His voice stirred me from my horror. I leaned forward and pitched my shoulder against Charlie's crucifix then, to lever the awful grave marker from the ground. It seemed like the least I could do for him, to erase in some small measure the bitter irony that my Orthodox Jewish father lay buried in heathen ground.

"What are you doing?" Daniel said, irritated.

"Charlie was a Jew, dammit! What's the matter with you?" And I wrenched the crucifix up and heaved it, like a track-and-field hammer, beyond the newly painted cemetery fence.

Daniel recoiled from my anger. He retreated around the rim of the cemetery and left its gate. He vanished up the dirt path, like I was a loose bull and he needed to ask Pastor Allen how to eject me.

I stared at Charlie's grave for a long time, as if for signs of life, like I waited for him to tell me what to do. A wave of malaria dizziness sat me down on his grave mound and another bad wave knocked me flat so I lay on top of him. The ground's cool dampness soaked through my shirt. I watched a pair of pure white egrets sweep across the cloudy dawn sky then and listened to monkeys, like brown naked insane men, shriek in dread to each other across the tops of the trees.

EIGHT

1

I lay on Charlie's grave morning and afternoon, listening to monkeys, birds, and antelopes, as the malaria resurfaced and burned through me, like dried sticks. The sheer array of weird animal noises—grunts, roars, brays, cackles, growls—seemed to mirror my own wild and fevery emotional fluctuations. I felt despondent, searing guilt at Charlie's death, that I might have, in fact, caused his heart attack, to relief that I'd never have to confront him that I wasn't Orthodox, to anger that even dead Charlie had once again hedged me into a truly lousy position, the predicament of having to telephone Vivian that he'd passed away.

The guilt was the toughest to bear, of course, the awful knowledge of my cowardice and its dreary outcome. Ah, what shame I felt! What shame!

Rationalizations crowded me also: Charlie would have died even had I stayed in Tanout; he was such a bully that I'd had the right to leave. I wept, cursed, implored forgiveness by turns. I vowed to change myself.

Nevertheless, it was simple cheek-reddening shame that burned through me as I lay on Charlie's grave mound, the stark perception that no matter how stupid the whole voyage, I'd been even more stupid to abandon my dad. Hell, I'd put up with him my whole life, why couldn't I have put up with him a few more months?

The sad afternoon wore on, the deep-toned church bell chiming off the hours. The sun was falling into the savannah's

rim of trees when Daniel and Pastor Harold Allen himself
came to visit me. The pastor was a short compact man in his
early fifties, wearing tortoiseshell glasses, pressed cotton
pants, and a polo shirt, with the brisk impatient manner of a
football coach before the big game.

Daniel introduced us.

"Pleased to meet you." The pastor leaned down and took
my loam-caked hand in his. "So sorry about your dad."

"Thank you." I watched him brush strands of yellow-gray
hair over a large bald spot. He had good clear skin and no jowls
or bags under his eyes, like Daniel, and I thought that he
might touch toes or do morning sit-ups, some old-fashioned
military exercise to vent his nervous energy.

"And I hear that you're feeling poorly, too." He was
cheerful and concerned though his gray eyes were cold behind
his lawyer glasses. He was sizing up my weaknesses, I figured,
an estimation that depended on how much babying I was
willing to take.

"Yes, I'm not feeling too well."

"And how about if we help you back up to the infirmary?
A bed has to be more comfortable than this cemetery dirt.
What do you say, Dan?"

I felt the strong pull of his will: his expectation that I'd
do as I was told. And why shouldn't I? The infirmary meant a
shaded room, a clean bed, hot food. It only meant getting off
of Charlie and letting myself be helped up the dirt path. But
something repulsed me about Harold Allen. Perhaps it was his
strong assumption that I'd obey him. Perhaps it was the
simple bland equanimity of his looks.

Daniel agreed, "Sounds good to me." He stepped forward
to help me up.

I might have returned to the infirmary, too, if the pastor's
manner and looks were all that irritated me. But there was a
gut-level aversion to the man that I couldn't quite define. I
imagined he only wanted me gone from the cemetery so he
could repair Charlie's grave cross, and so I shoved away
Daniel's hands and lay back down on Charlie, saying, "No,
no, no."

The pastor wiggled his glasses up on his pug nose. He

asked me, sharp edge entering his voice, "What's going on, Murray? Got some pain?"

"My father was an Orthodox Jew. He didn't like crucifixes."

"And you're afraid that if you leave the cemetery I'll stand it back up."

"Yes."

"Don't worry. We respect the dead."

"I think I'll stay here anyway."

"Leave him, Dan," the pastor said, and snapped his fingers to call my uncle back.

Daniel backed away from me. He resumed his place behind the short man.

I was irritated that Daniel responded so quickly to the pastor's command, like he was his houseboy. And I began to understand my ill will against Harold Allen: he used his religion so people would obey him, like a bad king—like I'd been Harlon Fitzwater's slave.

"We didn't know your family felt that way about crucifixes." He tried squashing the irritation in his voice to be a good sport. "If Dan or I had suspected . . . well, we wouldn't have put it up, right Dan?"

Daniel agreed. "Certainly not."

I stayed mad that my uncle brownnosed the pastor, that he felt his peaceful life was worth being this manipulative pastor's yes-man. Maybe that's why he never worked as more than a hardware store clerk after Toys Galore. Maybe that's why he hiked away from Rachael's grave.

"Okay. You stay here and mourn your father as long as you wish." The pastor gave in to me. "We realize this is a tragic time. But I'd like you to come to the mission office and call your mother. You'll tell me what arrangements she wishes to make."

That sounded all right and I said, "Fine."

Daniel clutched my fingers in one of his calloused workman's hands and help me stand. I wiped fever sweat from my brow, dusted off my shorts and shirt. I regripped my uncle's hand as we trailed Pastor Allen up the dirt path, past Daniel's church and circle of huts, to a cinder block building where

Patty Allen worked in a spartan office of metal folding chairs, fluorescent light, and a floor fan that scattered humid air about the room. She started at my appearance.

"Murray knows about his father," the pastor explained. "He's come to telephone his mom."

"I'm so sorry, Mr. Orloff."

"Call me Murray," I said to her, and slumped into a chair by a vacant desk. I rested my head on my folded arms, like an exhausted student, and counted cracks in the floor tiles, listened to the fan and buzzing fluorescent light.

Pastor Allen asked me for my telephone number in Israel; he spoke French to the international operator, his back to all of us.

Patty exclaimed, "How terrible this is."

I glanced up, thinking that she'd addressed me, but she only stared at Daniel who leaned against the doorframe. What I saw between her and my uncle, though, was a lover's glance, an intense naked gaze like the R-rated movies I'd sneaked midnight peeks at so many years ago in Holiday Inns that my family stayed at on our treks across the United States. The look was brief yet so very clear it confused me. At first, I thought it a hypersensitivity from my malaria until I remembered Daniel's sleep-talking—"Oh, Patty!"—of the night before.

Their look evaporated as soon as Harold Allen turned around. "The operator will call back in ten minutes when she's made the connection," he said. "But in the meantime, Patty and Dan, why don't we give Murray a chance to gather his thoughts?"

The three left the office. I rested my forehead back on the desk, waiting for the phone to ring, astounded at Patty Allen's leer at Daniel. What could her attraction for my humpbacked uncle be? How could the pastor not have noticed? The answers, however, seemed self-evident: Patty was attracted to Daniel for his easygoing manner; the pastor hadn't noticed the relationship because he didn't think Daniel man enough to cuckold him. Maybe my uncle's passivity or the cleric's exercise of his authority acted as smoke screens. Who knows? Maybe his pastoral zeal was the root of the affair, that he treated his wife as just another sheep in his flock. The telephone rang. The operator spoke in French, through heavy static. "*C'est Murray Orloff?*"

"*Oui.*"

"*Continuez, Iz-ray-el,*" she said, and hung up.

"Hello?"

"Hello?" I heard my mother say, her voice hollow and far away, like from beneath ground.

"Mom?"

"This is Vivian Orloff," Mother said.

Static pulsed through the line.

"It's Murray!"

"Murray?"

"Yes, Murray!"

"Murray!" She was so happy to hear from me. "Where are you, darling?"

"In Togo, at Uncle Daniel's."

"So you found him," Mother said. Her voice went flat, and I remembered how she disliked him.

I tried, "He asked after you and the kids."

"Tell him the kids are fine." She was curt.

"I'll tell him."

"And how about your father?" she asked. "Is he there?"

I massaged my temples with my fingers; I wanted badly to hang up.

"Murray?"

"Yes, Mom."

"I asked, where's your father?"

"He's not here," I said, hoping I could hang up before I had to tell her.

"I suppose he doesn't care to speak to me," Mother joked. Static dulled her voice to small electric pops, like a bug zapper.

"No, no, no, he certainly *would* care to speak with you. It's just that . . ."

"Just what?"

"It's just that . . ." I began, but lost the heart to stall any longer. I said, "Charlie's passed away, Ma."

"Charlie's what?"

[107]

"Charlie's dead!"

"I thought you said, 'Charlie's dead.' " Her voice was nervous, tinny.

"Yes, yes, that's what I said—Father's dead." And I waited, my eyes shut tight in the palm of my hand.

"Oh my dear God," Mother finally said. "Dear God."

"I'm so sorry, Ma." My body shook as I cried. I let out little gasps. My eyes teared into my palm.

"Dear God."

The office fan squeaked as it pivoted, rustled papers on the desks.

"How?" Mother asked. "When?"

"A heart attack four months ago."

"And he's buried *there*?" She started weeping.

Static coursed through the line. Mother gathered herself during the long pause. When the line cleared, she explained that our economic situation was terrible as usual. There was simply no money for a plane ticket home and I'd have to make my own way back to Jerusalem as quickly and safely as I could. Charlie, God forgive us, would have to remain buried at the mission.

I nodded my head as she spoke. My eyes were wet in the tears smearing my palm.

She finished speaking, "Do you understand me, Muz?"

"Yes."

And there was a long pause where everything settled in for us: Charlie's death, renewed contact with each other, Mother's command for me to return home. She wished me farewell in the traditional Jewish parting of mourners then, "Have simchas, my son." Have joy.

2

I hung up the phone and wiped my eyes with my hands. I steadied myself against the office's doorframe and lurched outside. The sun was a pink line in the rim of trees. I heard a truck. Pastor Allen, Patty, and Daniel waited for me at the bottom of the stairs. "She doesn't have the money to take him home," I mumbled to them.

"My Lord, he looks awful, Harold! Why are you letting him go back to that cemetery?"

"How can I stop him?" he asked. "He's a grown man. He does what he likes."

"*You* get him to go to the infirmary, Dan," she said. "You're his uncle."

"I'm afraid I don't have any influence with Murray," Daniel answered. "Hey, I hardly know the kid at all."

I swayed with dizziness. Patty gripped my bicep to steady me. She tried again to convince the two men to force me into the infirmary. I grew madder and madder. I thought Daniel's remark—"Hey, I hardly know the kid at all"—immensely callous, his attempt to shun all responsibility for me. He should have remained in the office after the pastor and his wife left and cried along with Vivian and me, I felt, at least faked some sadness for his brother's death. I mean, who did Charlie die for if not him? Instead, Daniel waited with the missionaries at the bottom of the office stairs and gummed his stogie casually around his mouth. It was like he'd never heard of Charlie and, by association, me.

"You're a jerk, do you know that, Dan?" I felt my anger welling inside me. "Your brother travels across the Sahara to make amends and save you from being a Jesus zombie, and you stand there making out like you've never heard of him and—" I leaned forward and took a swing at him, but Patty yanked my arm.

Daniel flinched. He stepped backward and thought better of a fight. "What a fool Charlie was for traveling here!" he said viciously. "How dare he think he could make amends when he caused my daughter to die. The louse. And I'm glad your father's dead, boy. Yes, glad! Only he should have croaked long ago, and not my little girl."

The pastor stepped between us. "Can't you see the boy's upset, Dan? What are you bothering him for?"

"He started it," Daniel said, and allowed himself to be pushed backward. He turned and disappeared past a thorn hedge.

"Don't listen to him, Muz." The pastor patted my shoulder. "Dan was just as upset about your father's passing as you."

"Bull."

"No, really, it bothered him. He told me so," Patty said.

"But these are for you," the pastor said, to change the subject, and handed me a bag of food, a blanket, and a mosquito net. "I'll stop by tomorrow to see how you're doing."

"I also packed a bottle of malaria pills," Patty listed, letting go of my bicep, "and a thermos of juice and umbrella for the sun."

"And I put a Bible in there also," the pastor said, "to comfort you in your grief."

"Thanks." The malaria pounded my temples. Chills raced up and down my spine.

"And make sure you read that Bible," Pastor Allen exhorted me. "It's a comfort."

"We'll talk about Jesus when you come visit, right?" I guessed.

"And God's ways to men," the pastor said. "What else really counts?"

3

It was nighttime when I weaved down the cemetery path, past Daniel's church and stands of leafy trees silhouetted in the full moon, back to Charlie's grave. I strung the mosquito net between the whitewashed fence and a crucifix grave marker, gulped down more malaria pills, and lay down on Charlie. I never imagined, given the circumstances, this might be disrespectful to him. It seemed the only way, however crazy, of communing with him. It was like I waited for him to advise me what to do next. I was, of course, shielding myself from my own pain, taking my mind off the awful conversation with my mother that made me too, too aware of the effects of my cowardice. Her sobs and throaty weeping, her "Oh my dear God," still burned in my ears.

But, naturally, nothing changed when I lay down, as a pea soup fog billowed into the cemetery and obscured the stars and constellations and turned the cemetery white as a steam room, as owls called to each other in ghostly hoots. The way my mother's voice cracked with my news, "Charlie's dead"— the tragic lilt of her grief—pierced my chest and bowels like bad pain and caused me to berate-curse-blame myself more than I already had. Our combined grief caused me to seek protection from myself, protection in the sense of spreading the blame for my mother's mourning: that her pain wasn't only *my* fault.

Thus my mind careened backward in alarm, like an addict searching frantically for his fix, for something to grab on to—to blame—that would make it easier to live with myself, racing back through Toys Galore memories and memories of the Berkshires, back across our moves throughout the United States and Israel. I found nothing unseemly in those circumstances to pin my guilt on, though, nothing that I didn't already know. Instead, I projected my thoughts forward to that fateful Sabbath dinner with the Dutch traveler, to our family supper at the lamb chop joint in downtown Jerusalem where Vivian demanded that I accompany Charlie, to buying a sleeping bag for the trip, the trip itself.

And I might not have come up with anything to pin the rap of Charlie's death on had it not been for my odd, spaced-out lucidity from the malaria pills, like being exhausted and drinking coffee to stay awake. For as I thought about money belts and Fun-Time tents, I also remembered Charlie's meeting with Rav Eliyahu, Jerusalem's famous expositor of Jewish law. I remembered how the rabbi refused Charlie his trip and how Charlie announced days later that he'd found a second rav to allow it. But since I'd seen Africa with its frequent coups and easy morality—everything, in short, was antithetical to Jewish sensibility—I didn't believe a second rabbi would permit this trip either, no matter how dishonestly Charlie posed his question. No, Charlie had lied to all of us. And at the core of this lie—for that is now what I truly believed it was—I saw Charlie's desperate retreat into the secular mentality he tried so hard to escape. His decision to pursue Daniel was an explicable but wrong lapse backward into his stage of impulsive decisions based on pure self-interest, a decision untempered by the divine wisdom he espoused for his family and textbook example of his chronic arrogance: it had been entirely too difficult for my father to accept that an old pale rabbi could know what was better for him than he himself.

What arrogance! What tragic lapse of principle and will! Daniel's retrieval from Baptist missionaries as Charlie's backhanded apology for canning his brother from the family business eighteen years ago and penance for his vicarious involvement in Rachael's demise, and the religious ideals of his life had fallen apart, his family scattered to the winds. One spurious reaction to a great rabbi's advice and exile! Death! One question of law! The gruesome fickleness of Charlie's lie and my own cowardice horrified me: a person could build and build his life and destroy it in one moment of insanity. If there was no divine law there was at least its need. Redeeming Daniel had been judged forbidden. Who had we been to disagree?

NINE

1

In the dark, foggy night, Charlie's lie froze me to his grave. Frustration and despair washed over me, like rain. That I was off the hook for his death proved cold comfort: Charlie was still dead and at this very moment my mother and siblings grieved. I say "frustration" because Charlie had so hidden his machinations that none of us ever had a chance of finding him out and preventing the trip. And as I lay beneath the mosquito net, crickets cheeping, small animals rustling through the brush, I marveled at my father's manipulations, at how far one man could justify and then follow a lie when he wanted something badly enough.

I sought justification for what he'd done: he wanted to make up with Daniel, he wanted to save a Jewish soul from Christianity. Yet I found this exercise in rationalization difficult, since I'd never wanted anything badly enough to lie or sacrifice a Toys Galore for it. This much I did understand: his pursuit after Daniel was not an idealistic one, rather his attempt to resolve the conflicts he'd been living with for twelve years. And so, ends justifying means, he lied to resolve those conflicts despite the fact that his lie contradicted his life's ideals as well. Charlie wouldn't have reasoned this out so straightforwardly. He was a practical and not philosophical man who relied heavily on his instincts. And since his instincts told him to journey after Daniel because this was surely the last chance he'd have to correct his wrongs, he went. The fact that he'd have to lie to pursue the voyage, that lies were against the Torah and everything he held dear, was no comment on the esteem nor the commitment with which he held his ideals. Ideals to my father were things to sacrifice for, even die for, but they weren't things to get in your way. All of which made Charlie's trip comprehensible but indefensible. It made me sad then angry then sad again, gave me a feeling of helplessness that froze me to his grave.

Pastor Allen and Daniel visited me the next morning, appearing beyond the cemetery fence. The sun had climbed above the savannah's rim of trees and burned away the fog, leaving the air misty and luminescent. The pastor held a big Bible. "Hey, how are you doing, Murray?" Rah-rah, once more the football coach. His words sounded distant because of my residual fever, like through a window.

"Better," I said. The shock of Charlie's lie was numbed this second by the sun and damp cemetery earth, monkey noises and humid plant smells, the slightly mind-altering effect of the chloroquinine pills.

"You strung up that net so nicely."

He'd praise those players, I thought, get them excited to go kick some ass.

Daniel frowned and hovered glumly behind the short man. I suspected Pastor Allen had coerced him to come, since the pastor wished to baptize me and required my uncle's presence to help his fundamentalist theology appear reasonable: if one family member could convert to Christianity then why in Christ's name couldn't I?

That Daniel showed up at all told me his hatred of Charlie wasn't as monumental as he made out yesterday. More likely, his attitude was like he told me at the infirmary: let bygones be bygones. He'd talked to me like that because I stupidly got him upset. Neither did I believe he was still angry about Toys Galore. Too many years passed for him to remain angry about a business that he'd left of his own accord. And yet I saw from Daniel's frown that he remained mad at Charlie. Someplace deep down, how could he not? I remembered the premonition I had the other night that he was withholding a secret from me, other news than Charlie's death, a secret that had something more to do with Orloff family history, but deeper and more personal than a job complaint, something amiss that Daniel still ached about and that, years later, was also part of what drove Charlie across the Sahara to his death, something whose shadow had appeared to us kids that fateful day in the Toys Galore warehouse.

"And Daniel told me that you were raised religious," the pastor went on. "How refreshing! What a pleasure to meet a young man who believes in God! A young man who knows what's important in life."

"What do you want from me, pastor?"

"I just want us to find comfort together, Muz." He smiled at me, lots of teeth.

"You mean, you want us to find Jesus together."

The pastor kept on smiling. How did he do it? "What greater comfort than Him?"

And while I held nothing against the short man for this conversion attempt—who understood religion's drives, passions, obligations, and obsessions better than I?—I was thinking of Daniel's frown and what must be my own sultry appearance, all in contrast to Pastor Allen's upbeat tone. But it wasn't just that we were glum together. My drugged clarity allowed me to glimpse more basic and more frightening similarities between us than those I'd imagined between myself and decrepit Winston Raymont. Daniel's volition, for instance, was tied to the pastor's will like mine had been tied to Charlie's. It was the same type of emotional bond that encouraged character immaturity, that hindered both of us from coping with the world and making our own decisions, a dependence that turned us into cowards. Indeed, the same cowardice that sent my uncle running away from his daughter's funeral sent me running away from my dad. I also saw how, with the possible exception of Max, each of us Orloff men was somehow misbalanced—Daniel with his indulgent self-pity, Charlie and his authoritarian self-interest, my own paranoid concern for my well-being. I mean—and I sighed loudly—why else were we all in varying degrees insensitive, selfish, or crude?

The pastor waited for me to answer him. Daniel hovered behind him, like a pouting Quasimodo.

The short man's owlish stare, his insistence. I felt a sudden desire to leave the cemetery, to be forever rid of my self-incriminations and this man's obnoxious presence.

And yet something held me to Charlie's grave. I located the feeling: my slight tendency toward responsible behavior stemming from delivering coup d'etat money and fighting with Harlon Fitzwater, decisions whose virtues (and ignoring the considerable folly that I might have been killed) were to get me to take care of myself, to show me that I could survive without my dad.

And while the memory of those lone, positive acts kept me that instant from hiking away from the cemetery, I recognized it as only a momentary stay. My athletic self-concern would quickly assert itself and propel me from the mission if I failed to reinforce this frail cycle of responsibility. Which is how I perceived, as Daniel gnawed a stogie to one side of the cheerful authoritarian pastor, that I'd reached the axis point in my psychological journey through Africa, an epiphany of moral choices: leave the mission immediately for home and never see Daniel again, or stay and help him. I figured, you see, that Daniel's days at the mission were anyway numbered. Despite the fact that he gave good service as the pastor's zombie, the short man wouldn't forget that Daniel was a Jew and that at his whim—a true-born Christian needing a job, the good pastor simply tiring of my uncle's looks—Daniel would be asked to leave. The mission certainly held no long future for Daniel. I also judged that for me to walk away from this situation smacked of that Orloff callousness I so wanted to avoid. Daniel was family and hurting and this should have been enough for me remain at the mission, debate theology with the pastor, and in this way extricate my uncle from his dingy life. My resolve wavered—what good resolves don't?— as I realized that any decision to help Daniel would require me to leap quantumly upward on the ladder of personal responsibility. I'd be assuming a commitment for a life other than my own. Which was ironic as I'd be fulfilling Charlie's crazy mission of extraditing him to Israel.

"Comfort together," I repeated the pastor's words aloud. The syllables were flat and hollow sounding, like my mother's voice on the telephone. Yet it was just this effect of distance that lent a hard-nosed objectivity to my Daniel decision, an objectivity that allowed me to perceive debate with the pastor as a great gift, as an opportunity to redeem myself somewhat by accomplishing Charlie's mission. So I ended my wavering and said, "Sure, I'd like some comfort."

"Wonderful," the pastor said, and hoisted his Bible from the cemetery fence. He walked through its gate. "First let's read from Jeremiah, chapter thirty-one."

I understood that he'd try to convert me by showing how Jesus fulfilled Old Testament messianic prophecies. I also understood that I'd need preparation if I was to debate him. It was five months since I attended yeshiva or read Charlie's pamphlet on how to refute Christian missionaries, and I asked Pastor Allen for the rest of the day to read through the New Testament he'd stashed with my food.

"Great." The pastor agreed happily, as if my perusal alone might be sufficient to convert me.

"And I'll need a pencil to take notes."

"Write anywhere you like," the pastor said, excited, and yanked a green mechanical pencil from his shirt pocket.

I swept aside the mosquito net to take it from him and noticed Daniel slipping away into the savannah's rim of trees. His complexion was unusually pale in the bright air and the expression on his face overly mournful, like an El Greco saint, as if he knew his time in Patty Allen's arms must soon come to an end.

2

I hiked out of the cemetery and sat in the shade of the clearing's treeline. My headache and fever were completely gone, replaced by a queer lucidity that catalyzed my epiphanies about Daniel and my responsibilities toward him. Presently, I sat between the roots of a leafy baobab tree and read about Jesus' rise and crucifixion. The story was pretty and tragic enough, like so many other Jewish lives. I was only surprised, as I noted contradictions from one gospel to the next, as I listed questions on the testament's back flap, that after my months and miles of travel and loss of Charlie, the talmudic dialectic came back so fast.

From time to time, I gazed up at the small, ordered cemetery with its whitewashed crucifixes and rectangle of flattened brown earth that was my dad. I wondered which of my parents' friends back in Massachusetts could have predicted that Charlie Orloff would come to his final rest in a bleak African grave. But maybe such news wouldn't surprise them. Hadn't they dismissed Charlie as a crank when we moved away?

And by way of contrast to those half-forgotten people in the Berkshire Hills, people who I recalled as wealthy and pleasant but spiritually dead, I pictured Mother, Louise, and Max, Orthodox as could be in Jerusalem, then Daniel and dirt-caked me scribbling notes in a New Testament margin. I wondered then, assuming that I was successful, what Daniel would do in Israel. But I came up with no answer except that Daniel, born a Jew, was better off living among Jews. Indeed, I thought, what would *I* do back in Jerusalem? How would I explain myself to family, friends, acquaintances, and my rabbis, people who would look at me in my Bermuda shorts and Hawaiian shirt like . . . like a heart attack? Yet to stay in Africa or emigrate to the United States were wilder notions, a retreat into those humanistic daydreams of total freedom that had only made my life a nightmare. No, eventually I'd have to return home. And so I perused the New Testament because I had no other options. And yet I didn't necessarily want to win the debate. How could I be thrilled with the prospect of taking care of Daniel? He was mercurial and unctuous and stank of cigar. It would be the *attempt* to win him back that would allow me to consider my familial duties fulfilled. For as I sat cross-legged between the steep roots of the baobab tree, I also realized that my present resolve to complete Charlie's mission was less that I wanted to become a mensch than that I was so damn tired of being a punk.

3

The tiny graveyard was cream white with thick fog when Pastor Allen and Daniel appeared at the cemetery gate. Each man gripped a large Bible, each a plastic lawn chair, an umbrella for the sun, a thermos, and bag lunch—provisions for a filibuster. The pastor, brisk and cheery, was dressed in green cotton pants and a yellow polo shirt. Daniel wore his khakis, a white oxford shirt, and even this early a stogie poked unlit out of his mouth.

The pastor unfolded his lawn chair ten feet away from me, dusted off its seat, and sat down. Daniel set up his farther away, one plot over and back, wiggling his rear end around the chair's cords where he sat, as if to find its sweet spot. Umbrellas and bags of food were stowed beneath the chairs; Bibles lay flat on laps.

I sat up on Charlie's grave mound, bunched up the mosquito net so it rested on top of itself, like a canopy, and sat cross-legged beneath it, Buddhalike. I combed my fingers through my long hair and beard. I peeled crusted loam from my cheeks with my dirt-blackened nails.

The pastor cleared his throat. He extended his condolences again. "You think you'll never recover but the Scriptures heal. The Lord comforts those who comfort themselves." And he closed his eyes. He clasped his hands over his Bible, leading us in prayer. "Dear Lord, grant us this day the courage and ability to discern Thy Truth. Let not pride nor desire blind our way. And let not the Tempter cause us to err. Give us the gift of Your Love, Jesus, that we may be saved in Your Holy Name. Amen."

"Amen," Daniel called.

Pastor Allen breathed deeply. He inspected me with his great gray eyes and I felt the strong pull of his will, his expectation that I'd be a good sport and accept what he said to be true.

The pastor puckered his lips and nodded at me. He directed me to Jeremiah, chapter thirty-one, like yesterday, and quoted the verses in a sonorous tenor, " 'Behold, the days come, saith the Lord, that I will make a new covenant with the House of Israel, and with the House of Judah. Not according to the covenant that I made with their fathers in the day that I took them by the hand to bring them out of the land of Egypt, which my covenant they broke.' "

The pastor interpreted the verses. "Notice, Murray, that God is promising Jeremiah that He'll make a new set of laws, a new covenant with man that will be the New Testament."

"But the five books of Moses says God's covenant is *forever.*"

"But Jeremiah is saying that there will be a *new* covenant," he insisted.

I ignored his mistake. I said sarcastically, hoping to show Daniel his adopted faith's stupidity, "Look, how about trying again?"

"Zechariah. Chapter nine, verse nine." The pastor turned pages in his Bible. " 'Rejoice greatly, O daughter of Zion. Shout, O daughter of Jerusalem. Behold the king comes to thee. He is just and victorious, humble, and riding upon an ass.' " The pastor explained, "These verses are a description of the first coming of Jesus Christ."

I said, "But Jesus was never king of the Jews!"

The pastor frowned. Daniel gummed his cigar from one side of his mouth to the other.

"Isaiah. Chapter seven, verse ten." The pastor flipped more pages.

I glanced over at Daniel and thought, how many people change their lives based solely on the truth or falsity of ideas? He drew on his stogie, unaffected by my sarcasm and theological verities. And who could blame him if he wasn't? What practical peace and contentment had I to offer him more than the pastor? I sounded angry now. Hell, I'd taken a swing at him back at the mission office. And I saw that I could say things as true as God and still he wouldn't follow me across a brook.

The pastor read from Isaiah.

My uncle crossed and recrossed his legs. I realized that no sense of ideal truth would ever affect this man. He exhaled blue smoke rings into the now fogless morning air—no ideas at all. He hated being here, and he gazed away from me with a studied indifference in various directions, as if trying to imagine havens of peace in the opaque air. His stupid remark— "Hey, I hardly know the kid at all"—came freshly to mind then. It made me itch to smack him across the face and I let the feeling swim over me. It felt good to be righteously angry, and I decided to take the offensive in the debate. I interrupted the pastor. "Hey, do you really believe in the New Testament literally?"

"One hundred percent."

"So you believe Matthew when he wrote that a Christian must give whatever he owns to any man who begs it of him?"

"Sure do." He smiled.

I quoted the verse I wanted. " 'Giveth to him that asketh thee, and from him that would borrow of thee, turn thou not away.' Do you believe this, pastor—honestly?"

"I said so, didn't I?"

"Then, please, I beg your shirt."

He kept grinning. He looked over at Daniel who looked quizzically back, and yanked out his shirttails. He lifted the shirt over his head and tossed it over to me. I thought, he's entirely too happy and maybe I should leak Daniel's affair with Patty, if I'd guessed right. But something held me back—what in God's name could that be? Maybe it was the pastor's smile that gave me the eerie feeling that I was somehow playing into his hands. Maybe it was just Daniel's lonely face, the stricken look that was taking hold of it like a nerve disease as the scene got uglier between the pastor and me. It made me halt, though, and not demand the pastor's pants. It made me see that he'd truly go all the way, letting himself be stripped naked to show allegiance to his cause, probably even letting me slap him around with that other verse, "Turn the other cheek."

The pastor watched me—he was eager to be stripped. His gray eyes were bright with the fire of his belief, his willingness to show off his convictions. And that was powerful—he was powerful. He might not argue theology well, but he didn't have to. He was a man suffering for his religion the great discomfort of living for years in the African bush. He had meaning, however misguided I thought it; he was like a peasant who lays down his plow and leaves family and friends when there comes the call to arms. And, frankly, how many of us are willing to do that? I respected the man for that—you had to. I saw that Daniel did, too. Meaning gave the short man heaviness—call it dimension—that wasn't found in most men simply because we live for our desires. It made his will felt and keen and ubiquitous, this commitment to cause. I wondered what would have happened between him and Charlie, another committed man. I imagined my father debating Pastor Allen in much the same way as me: stripping him naked and slapping him around. Charlie would have turned to Daniel and made cracks like, "Hey, Dan, isn't this stupid? Just get a load of this silly man. How can you believe in this crap?"

And yet, why would Daniel have allowed Charlie's abuse to affect him? He'd invested too many years in the mission for it to be severed by one unfortunate encounter. He'd look at the naked pastor, at smirking Charlie, and wish his younger brother gone—I'm sure of it. He'd be impressed with the pastor's commitment; he'd be impressed with how little Charlie had changed over the long course of his religious career. The same selfish, angry, vindictive man. There'd be absolutely nothing about Charlie that would attract Daniel: he'd stay put in the mission and Charlie would have to trek back to Israel without him. All of which showed me, as I stopped abusing Pastor Allen, that I was acting like Charlie would have acted. I was sarcastic and aggressive because Charlie would have been sarcastic and aggressive. I'd been willing to strip that man naked and hit him simply because he pissed me off, and wasn't this unconscionable? Charlie would have given in to his anger, also. He wouldn't have been sensitive to what Daniel needed. It would have been enough in his mind to vanquish the enemy, let the chips fall where they may. If Daniel couldn't see for himself—if he didn't have eyes in his head that this short man was a fake—well, perhaps it wasn't worth taking him out of here at all. He was a zombie, the slave of a zombie. This is what Charlie would have thought and sounded like. He would have shown Daniel how misguided his involvement with the mission was and so boxed him into a corner; he wouldn't have given Daniel the dignity of his own choice because he didn't trust him to make the right one. It was totalitarian, arrogant. I thought, and isn't that how he'd always treated his wife and kids?

The pastor finished reading Isaiah. "So what do you think of that, fella?"

"A great prophet," I said, absentminded, but not as a joke. I stared at my shrinking, wallflower uncle now. I felt the still-cool air and smelled the grass.

And I saw that to help Daniel I needed to evolve beyond Charlie's negativity, that vicious cycle of mistrust and bossiness that had so alienated me from him. It was essential for my uncle but even more for me since I'd always remain my father's son, and why should my personality be better than his? Why wouldn't I also be despotic with my own wife? Such lousy personality traits and their too-tangible effects scared me. I didn't want and hoped to God that I wouldn't repeat my father's life mistakes. Which would be easy as boiling water to do: easy to follow my angry desires right now, easy to humiliate this short man. I'd be appealing to Daniel from the very worst part of me, the part I'd inherited from Charlie and which Daniel (and I) had run away from.

For what Daniel needed now was not ideas but love. It's what he'd been missing all these years and what he didn't get from the pastor or his wife. Harold Allen gave him the grand picture of a man willing to die for his beliefs; Patty gave him some personal attention, some sex. She'd never leave the mission to elope with Daniel, though—the test if there was truly love between them—and I was sure that he must know this. He must know that they considered him once and always a Jew, as a man who'd remain forever beyond their pale.

The pastor read from Micah and interpreted. "And how about that one?" he asked.

"Another great prophet," I said, able to refrain from saying that I thought his interpretations forced and without contextual accuracy, in fact really stank. For I'd decided, crazily, taking up the gauntlet of Charlie's mission, that I wanted Daniel to come to Israel with me: there was no future for him here, but none.

The pastor wanted a better answer from me. "Is that all you have to say?"

I managed to keep my mouth shut.

Daniel noticed my self-control.

And I realized that the power to affect someone, religiously or not, came in direct proportion to giving up your power to coerce.

Daniel watched me. I watched him back, feeling my anger. But I called it Charlie's anger now: I didn't have to feel it if I didn't want.

Monkeys shrieked to each other. The sky was a Bombay blue and suddenly filled with white herons.

"Murray?" The pastor was shirtless, still eager.

I decided to kill the disputation. "I want to apologize, Pastor, for being so pompous before."

This caught him by surprise. He sat back in his lawn chair. "Why, why, that's quite all right."

"And I want to apologize to you also, Uncle Daniel, for trying to punch you yesterday."

"Don't worry about it, boy. You were just upset from talking to your mother," he said, and leaned forward, elbows on knees, interested.

I addressed the pastor. "You'll excuse me if I end the debate. You're not going to convince me nor I you and all we'll do is hate each other more than already."

"But I love you, Murray, truly," he said. "And Jesus loves you."

"And I believe that you do, Pastor, but only impersonally. You love me for what I could become, for what you could do for and with me. Which is certainly better than most men." I watched my uncle puff his cigar. I still felt anger in me and sighed in the warming air. "But I want to talk to my uncle a moment, Pastor." I could hear the control in my voice. "Uncle Daniel, if my father were alive I know that he'd want to apologize to you for everything that happened at Toys Galore. He'd want to apologize for Rachael—"

"Crap." He glared at me.

"He felt bad about everything for many years," I went on calmly. "The proof is that he tried hard to come see you and that he died in the attempt."

Daniel was quiet. I waited for him. "He felt bad?"

"Very bad," I said. "It's just that Charlie was a bad talker."

"What's that mean? He had bad grammar?"

"For instance, he never told Louise, Max, or me that he loved us. He never said he was sorry when he was wrong, and yet he was sorry."

Daniel nodded. "Feelings were hard for him."

"Please, Uncle Daniel," I appealed, "let me apologize to you on my father's behalf. Let me ask complete forgiveness from all the real and perceived bad that he did to you. Let me ask you from the very bottom of his heart."

I waited. The wind lifted the mosquito net canopy. The wide green baobab leaves quivered at the savannah's rim of trees.

Daniel leaned back in his chair and clamped his hand over his eyes. He sat still a long time. I imagined that he was struggling with his own bitterness like I'd struggled with my anger, finding out if it was within himself to let go in one moment the hatred that he'd been living with for years.

The pastor's head was bowed over his open Bible. I pinched up between my thumbs and forefingers some damp earth from Charlie's grave.

Daniel finally opened his eyes. They were teary and red rimmed. He cried hoarsely, in that voice smoky from years of stogies and Scotch, "I forgive you, Charlie!" And he put his hand back over his eyes and wept silently. The pastor and I watched him cry.

He finished. He dried his eyes on the sleeve of his white shirt. He looked at the pastor and then hard at me, as if to ask, what now?

I inched forward on Charlie's grave. I put my feet out and stood into the sun. There was nothing else to ask forgiveness for. The only question that remained was where were we going from here? And so I said to my uncle to give him what he truly needed, not sure that I meant it but not sure that I didn't either, "I love you, Uncle Daniel." And waited for him to absorb this, to understand that I had nothing at all to gain.

"But why?" That good question.

"Because you're family—what better reason than that? Other people in Israel love you, also."

"I'm not so sure about that," he said cryptically.

"But *I* love you."

"Even though I'm Christian."

I wanted to say, you're not really a Christian, you'll give it up like a worn suit once you leave this place, but I said sincerely, hearing again my self-control (and hoping he didn't), "Even though you're a Christian."

Which impressed him. Which made him stop looking at me hard. Even the pastor glanced up then.

"And I want you to come back to Israel with me," I continued. "I want you to be part of the Jewish people, however Christian you are. I want you to be part of my family's life. I can't offer you the chance to build a church and I can't even say that it will be as peaceful as here, especially when someone you like as much as Patty makes you food and sees that you're so comfortable and stuff." I wanted to allude to her, hoping in light of his forgiveness of Charlie—his ability to master his own hate—that he'd have the wisdom to see his affair with her couldn't last forever, even much longer, and that he was fooling himself to think the pastor wouldn't find out or that he'd eventually have to leave this mission for another reason anyway. But that's all I could do—allude. I didn't want to accuse him and have the pastor curse him out and order him to leave, because then I'd lose him that way: he'd drift away from me, drift somewhere else and roost, and I'd have won the battle and lost the war. And, still, I think my allusion would have escaped my uncle had it not been for the way the pastor picked up on it, the incongruity of mentioning his wife here at all.

He stared at me and then Daniel, suspecting. Daniel folded back within himself as the missionary weighed his own paranoia.

I repeated my offer. "Come to Israel with me, Daniel. What future is there for you here?"

He sat lost in thought.

"Are you going to get married?" I pressed him. "Are you going to build another church?"

The pastor stood suddenly and wrung his hands. He marched to the cemetery gate and back, then stood in front of my uncle, legs akimbo, hands on his hips, like a drill sergeant. He'd counted on a debate where he could show his love of

Jesus and all he'd gotten were apologies, tears, and the clue that Patty was sleeping around. He asked, "Daniel, are you having an affair with my wife?"

Daniel leaned back as if punched. He glanced over at me and then away—but how in the world could I know?—then back at the pastor, into his lap, at the ground in front of his feet. I thought, so it's true. You could see it. And still the pastor might have dismissed this hint of wrongdoing—you had to be listening real well to have caught it—but he'd seen Daniel grow these past minutes with his forgiveness of Charlie and grow away from him when he entertained my offer to come to Israel. Which was a hell of a note after he'd taken such good care of this poor slob. Which is why, perhaps, the pastor could finally suspect his wife with Daniel and when Daniel fell off his pedestal of good slave, when the short man asked again, "Is it true, Dan?"

Daniel chomped on his stogie. He stared at the ground and shook his head over his predicament. I thought he might hike out of the cemetery then, like at Rachael's funeral, but he stood still.

"Dan, tell me it's not true." The pastor's voice softened. He was trying to make it easier for Daniel to come clean or to lie. "Just say it's not true and I'll believe you. A hundred percent."

But from the way Daniel slouched and kept staring at the ground, the way he quit chomping on his cigar, I knew that I'd guessed right about Patty and him, and I saw that the pastor also knew. We only waited now to see if Daniel would tell the truth or lie.

My uncle's face wrinkled up from his thoughts. "I can't, Harold." And Daniel watched my father's grave, as if dead Charlie who had forced him to forgive had now forced him to say the truth.

The pastor's frown deepened. He fussed with his glasses. He smoothed his blond-gray strands of hair over his bald spot. "How could you, Dan?" he asked, his voice soft and pained, "I took care of you—"

"You take care of yourself, Harold!" Daniel blurted out.

"You stuff your discipline down everyone's throat. And if they are weak people, like me, you have contempt for them."

"I gave you life!" the pastor claimed, in horror.

"You despised me!" Daniel answered back. "You tolerated me because I built you a church."

"You were my brother in Christ—"

"Ah, Harold," Daniel said, but calmly now, like he felt sorry for the man.

The pastor hooked his thumbs through his belt loops. He kicked at the cemetery grass, like a cowboy, waiting, it seemed, for Daniel to repent or say that everything was a lie. But there was only heavy silence in the sunny graveyard, crucifix shadows falling across the clipped grass, the monkeys quiet in the trees.

The pastor turned away wordless from Daniel, one hand dropping forlornly from his belt loops and then the other. He opened the cemetery gate and began trudging up the church path.

Daniel tossed the stogie from his mouth. He scratched his nose and nodded glumly, like he'd expected this all along. His long arms dangled over the sides of his lawn chair and he looked at me from over the rims of his pince-nez, but not spitefully, as if I were only an effect and not the cause of his problems.

Daniel sighed. I sighed, too. Tree leaves flapped in a humid breeze. Gray clouds blew through the gorgeous sky. Which is when the final awful Orloff family secret came to me—the reason for Daniel's discomfort when he told me his sad tale in the infirmary and his cryptic comment, "I'm not sure about that"—when he understood that I was bringing him back into the orbit of his family and past life but with love and respect, giving him the dignity of his free will—why Vivian called Daniel a wimp, why Charlie had to lie, why all those years ago in the Berkshires my family never socialized with his: once I acknowledged that Daniel and I were more similar than Charlie and me. For I wed Daniel's affair with Patty Allen to Vivian's ancient dislike of him and her great reticence to allow Charlie to pursue his tragic Saharan quest, and I finally understood. "There was once something between you and my mother, wasn't there, Dan?"

Daniel watched me steadily over the tops of his pince-nez. Parrots cackled about us; the white crucifixes surrounded us like a platoon. "Vivian used to be my wife."

PART IV

♦

The Trip
Home

TEN

Uncle Daniel and I peered at each other a long time in the tiny cemetery. His eyes were red and glassy behind his pince-nez, his complexion ashen. I had no illusions that he noticed me at all, occupied as he must have been with visions of my mother. Certainly his last confidence had cost him much, as certainly there must be significant embarrassments and tears, betrayals of all kinds darkening that period of his life. And while I didn't doubt my uncle for a second—no one could fake his ghastly stare, the pallor of his cheeks—I simply couldn't imagine him married to my mom. Vivian wore bright orange lipstick and smoked Kools and screamed at managers of department stores, even in Jerusalem. Daniel was retiring by nature, self-concerned, pliant. He coped with problems by literally running away.

"So what happened between you and my mom, Dan?" I finally asked, meaning their divorce. And though it was prob-able no one alive besides Daniel's ex-wife Estelle knew about the brothers' love triangle or whatever it was, I also reflected how, being suppressed, the particular horrors of the story must have worked their constant bitter way throughout my uncle's system, like lymphatic cancer.

But if Daniel was pained to admit "Vivian used to be my wife," I was also pained to hear it. It was one thing to learn of a parent's mistakes in the service of a higher good—for in-stance, Charlie's lie to make up with Daniel—and quite another to learn of a parent's misconduct via passion. Need-less to say, their whole entanglement felt palpably sordid, much like Daniel's affair with Patty Allen. And the realization that my long, nightmarish trip through Africa had its seeds in the misactions of three adults thirty years or so before, felt worse.

Nevertheless, Daniel's confession about Vivian shocked me only dully, because since Rachael's death and Daniel's resignation from Toys Galore weren't Charlie's fault, I figured that there must be a more festering wrong between the brothers to drive Charlie to Africa for Daniel. And so "Vivian used to be my wife" came to me as news of only a surprising inevitability, a shock stripped of its raw ability to awe. But I also recognized Daniel and Vivian's failed union as a potentially damaging image to me, damaging to my memory of Charlie and my future relations with my mom. I deemed it healthier therefore to know the facts of their history rather than feign their ignorance. Which is what forced me to ask my uncle, "So what happened between you and my mom, Dan?"

I say "healthier" because from the moment I forsook my religion for Mr. Fitzwater's humanism, I'd felt disoriented. My religious beliefs were branded by him as racist, and I'd tossed aside my world of ritual for his flag of tolerance. The fact that I hadn't acted in consonance with that humanism, for example my descent like a Harpy into Daniel's life, had further disoriented me, stranding me in a moral no-man's land where I shunned Judaism because of its restrictions yet understood that all my newfound openness had led to a certain personal disintegration. Thus I came to demand a knowledge of my father's sordid affairs because those details would be more real to me than anything else, real in the sense that they would flesh out Charlie Orloff who was my standard of behavior and who I always reacted strongly against. For no matter how scandalous Father ended up seeming to me, it was a moral reaction, or repugnance, I sought now, a reaction with enough power, like a megaton bomb, that might compel me to transform my attenuated life.

And though Daniel could easily have told me to get lost, that such history was none of my business, he leaned back in his lawn chair and cleared his throat. I saw that he was going

[134]

to tell me about his marriage to my mother, as well as the guts of it. Perhaps he figured my Saharan trek and indignities suffered at the hands of Mr. Fitzwater as well as Charlie's tragic death entitled me to an understanding of the historical forces at work in my life simply because I was their victim. Perhaps Daniel simply needed to tell his story without suppression, like to a stranger in a bar.

Daniel, at any rate, folded his arms across his chest and crossed his legs. He broke the seal on a fresh stogie and stared reflectively into the bib of trees as birds zipped over the crucifixes, as the asphyxiating noontime humidity gripped us, like skin.

"The first time I saw Vivian was at Avaloch in the summer of 1948," Daniel began. Avaloch was an old country inn located in Lenox, Massachusetts, in the Berkshire Hills. "I'd recently graduated with a degree in history from Williams College, thanks to the GI bill. I'd worked as a quartermaster in the Philippines during the war. And the very summer that I met Vivian, I'd decided not to pursue a Ph.D. in history and join my father's wholesale toy business instead.

"But I remember the evening we met distinctly: a Saturday night in the first week of August, during a hot spell. The sky was clear and the stars were out. A yellow moon hovered above the dark trees. I was dressed in white linens. I was tall and slender then. My back was still pretty straight."

"And where was Charlie?"

"Charlie was stationed in Staten Island throughout the war. He stayed there afterward and worked as a welder in a shipyard," Daniel explained. "But he fancied himself a painter, and whenever he visited Old Joe and me in Lenox after the war, he dressed in black turtlenecks and berets, like a bohemian. He grew a goatee—"

"And always kept it," I added, remembering how Charlie paced the gravelly plains outside our Fun-Time tent on the night that he lectured me about my Jewish duties, his goatee bent like a shrub in the Sahelian wind.

"Anyway, I parked my Chevy and walked toward the bar, called The Five Reasons. I could hear the crickets and the black jazz all at once—Avaloch was hip, you know." He paused to adjust his pince-nez and comb his fingers through his gray bangs, as if he wanted to look good for the memory of Vivian. "And there she was, still in culottes and a halter top from the daytime," he said, more excited than I'd seen him yet, the image of their first meeting vivid to him unlike any other episode in his life except, alas, Rachael's death. "A big blond dame with shocking orange lipstick. You could spot those lips from fifty paces. She was dozing in an Adirondack chair near the bar entrance. A smoking cigarette dangled from her lips." Daniel nodded, happy at his recall of the details. "She was unlike anyone I'd ever seen in Lenox. Beautiful and exotic, tough looking, the type of broad who would get into a knife fight with another woman to protect her man."

I tried imagining my mother, who for the last eight years had run a small branch post office in the Old City of Jerusalem where she weighed packages and glued stamps, in a desperate knife fight with some floozy over my Uncle Daniel with his humpback and smelly stogie, and I almost laughed.

"Needless to say, I didn't know how to approach her," Daniel confessed. "She seemed so . . . so . . . worldly that she intimidated the hell right out of me. I wanted to ask her for a cigarette, to start a conversation with her, but she was napping. So I just stood there like a dummy and gawked at her. People sauntered in and out of the bar and snickered at me like I was some Peeping Tom. I hoped the jazz might wake her up, or the noise of people flirting over the loud music. Finally, I became too embarrassed to stand there any longer, and I just kicked her sandals with my loafers, like you might shoo away a cat.

"And slowly, Vivian opened her eyes. Smoke from her cigarette curled past her nose and over her blond hair. She stared at me in my white linens, through this veil of smoke, like she was a Gypsy lady about to divine my future. 'Who are you?' she asked me, but familiar-like.

"Her eyes were hidden behind the tobacco smoke and the glare of the yellow fog lights. I didn't have a clue how to answer her question, and for one unending, unbearable moment I listened to the hot jazz and people's voices above the loud music. I watched moths, their wings singed from the fog lights and no longer able to fly, walk over her blond hair.

"Any good timing for a witty response had long passed. I wanted more than anything to impress this woman, but I wasn't a witty man by nature, and surely she'd heard all the lines. But she obviously wasn't from the Berkshires, and folks, at least in the forties, didn't come to Lenox for escape from entanglements—they came for romance. So I decided to gamble on that: I tugged my hands out of my white trouser pockets and stepped near her so that my legs straddled her legs. I leaned forward and placed my fists on each arm of her chair. I looked her straight in the eye and said to her, as intensely as I could, 'I am the man you've always been waiting for.' "

Daniel grinned at me sheepishly over the whitewashed crucifixes. His humpback towered above his grin, and the pince-nez perched at the end of his crooked nose made him resemble a vulture. "Corny line, eh, Muz?"

"Pretty corny," I agreed from beneath my canopy, stretching out my legs on Father's grave and leaning on my elbows, as if Charlie were a divan—my vain attempt to look casual after learning that my mother slept around before she married my dad.

"At least I was sincere," Daniel defended himself. "At least *I* believed my corny line. Anyway, Vivian placed her hand against my chest and shoved me away. I backed away from her, and my cheeks flushed red as I waited for her to tell me off. She even yanked her cigarette from her mouth and said, 'You've some nerve—' But she broke off when she noticed me blushing, like she remembered this was a summer evening in the Berkshires and not Flatbush.

"After that, she sat still in her Adirondack chair and watched me. All those moths with the singed wings crawled over her thick blond hair and made it look alive, like she was Medusa. And she seemed to decide something in our endless first gaze, maybe that I wouldn't hit her or cheat on her like Brooklyn boys did. Which is when she visibly warmed to me. And, as if to make up for lost time, she shook off one of her sandals and ran a bare foot with its orange toenails up my argyle socks, onto my bare calf. 'Could be, nice boy, could be,' she said in that deep sexy voice of hers, to reencourage me."

I pressed my hands over my ears. "Stop it!" The image of Daniel flirting with Vivian—that my religious mother should encourage a man besides my father—horrified me like a betrayed confidence. Mother had always been our guardian angel, protecting us kids as best she could against Charlie's onslaughts, repressive schoolteachers, the world-at-large— how could she have done such an awful thing? But with Daniel's version of Orloff family history came the insight that my parents' moral backgrounds were similarly shady, and this upset me. In light of Charlie's lie I wanted—needed—Mother to be my moral rock of Gibraltar and not a victim of her whims and passions like Charlie had been, like myself.

Daniel stopped his narrative and rekindled his stogie. I thought he smirked behind the bluish smoke. Perhaps he was pleased to get a rise out of me—a sort of twisted vengeance for what I'd caused him. Still, all said and done, I believed knowledge of my parents' and Daniel's past would help me put my own life together, and so I uncovered my ears to hear the unhappy sordid rest of the story. Daniel took my cue and described their courtship.

The couple saw each other every day in August 1948, and on into September, until Daniel started to work for his dad as a wholesale toy salesman. Then he was on the road daytimes. Often, he slept overnight in Poughkeepsie, Rochester, Syracuse. As Daniel put it, the frustration of suddenly not being able to be together caused him and Vivian to marry, as if legalizing their relationship could somehow bring back their euphoric August weeks.

Yet Old Joe, Charlie and Daniel's father, opposed the match. He referred to Vivian as "that Brooklyn slut" and refused to attend their December wedding at Avaloch. "Which, frankly, bugged the hell out of me," Daniel said, "and still does. I mean, here I am busting my rear for that old coot, and he doesn't even have the decency to come to my wedding!"

But Old Joe didn't halt at mere disapproval. He actively attempted, or so it seemed to Daniel, to sabotage the union.

He sent Daniel on the road six days a week and still refused to meet Vivian. And three months after the nuptials, their marriage was on the rocks. Vivian demanded that Daniel leave the toy business or she'd leave him. And it was here that Daniel proved himself a spineless man: he opted for the toys.

"I begged her to calm down, to tough it out a few more months," Daniel explained. "Then I could inform Old Joe that I paid my dues and to lay off of me. But what I never came to grips with, and what Vivian always said, was that the old coot would never ease up on me as long as I was married to her. He thought her plebeian and unrefined, as if we Orloffs were the landed gentry." Daniel threw up his arms in dismay. "Maybe my old man hated New Yorkers. I don't know. But Vivian couldn't compromise either because she was so miserable—" Daniel broke off his sentence and gazed at me sorrowfully. The catastrophe was like yesterday to him; I saw that he wanted my empathy—more love—for all his rotten luck.

"Yes, what a shame that was," I said, quite happy Daniel wasn't my father. In fact, I felt palpable relief when my sense of the story's progression told me that at the end of his tale he wasn't suddenly going to turn out to be my biological father. Yet still, it was weird for me to perceive Daniel's pain and feel benefited by it, the relief that Charlie was my father and not him. But as I needed to hear the rest of the past, I managed to nod and add, "It's too bad Old Joe had it in for Vivian."

"And I simply didn't find it in myself to be decisive," Daniel went on. "I wanted my marriage *and* the security of the toy business." He shook his head again, amazed that he'd expected such fantasy. "And so I postponed the decision until it was too late: she left me." He banged his stogie hand on his chair's arm in regret; ash from his cigar floated to the ground. "How she despised me!" he cried out, echoing about the clearing. "How I despised myself!"

Daniel and my mother were divorced four months after they married, in March 1949. Harry Truman was president; Mao Tse-tung would win his Long March that year. Vivian, too depressed to return to her family in New York, moved to North Adams, a small mill town in the northern Berkshires, where she found a job as a waitress and rented an apartment with the alimony Daniel paid her monthly through his lawyer, Edwin Cooke.

"And I never went to North Adams to try to get her back!" Daniel exclaimed, newly surprised at his foolishness. He stood from his chair and paced to the cemetery's far end, like the pastor had, perhaps to expend his bad feelings. "At first I was too angry to try to get her back. Then the toy business became very good and I rationalized to myself that she wasn't 'suitable,' like Old Joe always said." Daniel hooted bitterly at the sharp irony of the word, thinking, I imagined, at how unsuitable everything else in his own life had been since then.

And it was not long after he divorced Vivian that he realized he'd made a big mistake, but he feared Old Joe too much to claim her back. In the meantime, he supported her generously. He was biding his time until some development in the family business—another company's lucrative buy-out offer or Old Joe's retirement—would allow him the freedom to court and with luck marry her again. Similar fantasies had separated them in the first place, and I didn't know how to account for this one either. Perhaps Old Joe's abusive personality prevented Daniel from ever developing an emotional independence that would have saved his marriage to Vivian.

Daniel sighed deeply in the humid cemetery. He stood behind a crucifix, hands resting on both sides of its crossbar, and said in his tobacco-raspy voice, softer but more intensely than before, "Then Charlie came home from Staten Island. The boatyards laid off people, and his wartime friends had scattered. And in spite of his beret and goatee, Charlie came to understand that he was no painter. And Old Joe, happy to have his sons near him, offered Charlie a job."

Daniel bounced his hands up and down on the grave marker, like he wanted to bang it into the ground.

"Once I realized that I made a mistake with Vivian, I became jealous of every man. I even suspected Edwin Cooke, my nice responsible lawyer who delivered my monthly alimony checks to North Adams, of a love interest in Vivian. Consequently, when Charlie moved back to Lenox, I transferred that responsibility to him. And . . . and the rest is history." Daniel faced away from me. All I saw was his stooped back. The green cemetery lawn and crucifixes fanned out to either side of him and the tangled savannah and unkempt bib of trees stretched out beyond him.

When Daniel faced me once more his eyes were again red, his complexion even grayer than before. "And exactly a year after Charlie started delivering my alimony, he announced to Old Joe and me that he was going to marry Vivian. Their whole affair was an utter shocking surprise, of course, and I was mortified. Old Joe ranted on about Vivian, even at work and in front of those ugly secretaries he always hired. Deep down, though, I think he was strangely pleased at Charlie's monumental *chutzpah*, that the apple hadn't fallen far from the tree. For propriety's sake, he could hardly approve, and he threatened Charlie with expulsion from the business. But Charlie called his bluff. He answered the old man, 'Well, you can just take your toy business and shove it all the way up you know where, Joe.' Then Charlie stalked out of the warehouse." Daniel chuckled appreciatively. "I always admired the hell out of your father for that, because I never, *never* could have said that to Old Joe myself, and I'd so wanted to."

"But then what happened?"

"Why Charlie married your mother and had you and the other kids."

"I mean with Old Joe."

"Old Joe backed down from his expulsion threat." He flashed angry again. "He drove to North Adams to retrieve Charlie and somehow made amends with Vivian. And the rest"—my uncle circled his stogie hand, a sour, dismissive gesture—"the rest *you* know." And while I didn't doubt the fact of his marriage to my mother—that was more than even he would lie or fantasize about—I was informed, finally, that Charlie's ancient kidney punch to Daniel, the blow that set him up for his strong guilt about Rachael and Toys Galore and sent him careening across the Sahara to his death, was his own marriage to Mother, the very relationship that I considered to be sacred in the eyes of God. And I was startled as I sat on my dead father's grave in the hot African sun, as Daniel narrated the denouement of his marriage to Vivian, that Charlie should risk his life and mine to retrieve this irresponsible, spineless brother of his, the first husband to his wife. Why hadn't he let this sleeping, Baptist dog lie?

I imagined two answers: first of all, Charlie considered our trek the correct moral choice, despite Rav Eliyahu's injunction. It was his skewed idea of redress for imagined wrongs committed against his brother. Or, second, perhaps Daniel's marriage to Vivian wasn't the torrid, circumstantially tragic affair my uncle made it out to be. Rather, theirs was a formally legal but loveless union, and Charlie traversed the Sahara for Daniel simply because Old Joe had once come and retrieved him from North Adams and he wished to extend to his long-lost brother this same family loyalty and chance for a fresh start in life.

Frankly, I didn't buy my second theory at all—that was *my* addition to the trip. It assumed a disinterested chivalry on Charlie's behalf and my father was too impulsive and brooding *not* to act out of an acute sense of self-interest or guilt. I also wondered what he'd thought about all those years ago when he drove Daniel's alimony check up U.S. Route 8 to North Adams and realized that he was in love with Vivian. Such an answer eluded me until I fathomed that the core of my elders' triangle stemmed from mere sexual attraction. I say "eluded" because passion and how it forever altered lives was something I didn't yet understand. For after my five months in Africa, I still hadn't had a woman. And only now as I listened to my uncle depict his marriage, and sensed the sexual underpinnings of my family's history were no anomaly, did I feel it odd that I'd never had a woman, especially in light of my friendship with Mr. Fitzwater. I rationalized my virginity, though, as the last thin mental thread that had kept me Jewish: keeping me at arm's length from the surrounding goyish culture and so allowing Charlie's lie to have its dissonant, introspective effect on me.

Another result of my quasi-moral thinking in this Baptist cemetery was the Jewish law issue of Daniel and Vivian's wedding. Had Daniel married my mother in an orthodox or civil ceremony—were they truly wed or considered as unmarried people living together? For if they were wed Jewishly, then Vivian wouldn't be allowed by Leviticus to marry her husband's brother. And, worse, her children from Charlie—Louise, Max, and I—would be considered bastards. And bastards in Judaism could marry only other bastards. And the offspring of our marriages would be bastards also, as would our children's children and their children after them forever: such a mistake was for keeps. And so when Daniel informed me that Vivian and he were married by a rabbi, I jumped up from Charlie's grave. Adrenaline coursed through me, like I'd been stung. You see, if I planned to marry a gentile woman and never return to Jerusalem, this bastard issue would never have worried me: my kids from such a marriage wouldn't be Jewish. But after all my miles and pain, I wanted a regular life and regular meant a Jewish wife and normal Jewish children simply because I was Jewish. Family life, however irreligious, would be easier that way.

Which is when I realized that I *had* to shlep Daniel back to Israel to find out the truth about his and my mother's marriage only because Vivian might distort her history to keep peace in the family. I realized, with no small displeasure, that Daniel actually entertained the idea of courting and remarrying my mom. I saw his mind remained whimsical after all these years, filled with nursery-like ideas of an anxiety-free life and romantic love, and the discomforts of a one-time northward trek across the Sahara wouldn't deter him from his fantasies: Uncle Daniel had nothing left to lose.

It was high noon in the square cemetery, and the day's humidity blanketed me in sweat. The monkeys started screeching again from the green sheet of trees, bloodcurdling yells. I halted my pacing and glanced back at my uncle—a blustery but gentle, very confused, humpbacked man who expected more and more of my sympathy and love like I'd wanted babying from Harlon Fitzwater. Which spurred on a last comparison of myself to Daniel, an epiphany that showed me in a startling way that my cowardice toward Charlie in Tanout was also fantasy thinking and that, like my uncle, I'd avoided moral decisions by literally running away.

Which gave me another real scare. Like the prospect I was

a bastard, this knowledge reinforced my doubts that my nature was more fundamentally akin to my uncle's than to my dad's. How easy it had been for me to run away. How easy it would still be for me to squander my life. And it was only this fragile scaffolding of reflective thought, initiated by Ruth's offer, catalyzed by Charlie's lie, kept alive by killing the debate with Pastor Allen and professing love for my uncle, by the tension of my celibacy, that prevented me from running away again and running now, which slowly, slowly, was extricating me from the quicksand of Mr. Fitzwater's humanism, whose banner of tolerance had atrophied my soul.

ELEVEN

In the hot noon sun I loosened the mosquito net over Charlie's grave. On hands and knees, I smoothed my arm- and footprints on his flattened mound: my attempt at last respects. Afterward, Daniel led me from the cemetery. At the church path, I gazed back. Despite my manicure, Charlie's grave still looked trampled. I was saddened to realize that Pastor Allen would certainly repost Charlie's crucifix over him and that no one in this savannah would ever appreciate what a tragic mistake that truly was. "Rest in peace, Charlie." It was all I could think to whisper to my father before I turned forever away.

I waited outside Daniel's hut while he packed his bags. The crabgrass yard stretched like a cheap pile carpet to a rusting metal flagpole where Patty Allen stood with her African women and children, the baby scales of her food program, her sacks of CARE grain.

Daniel emerged from his cottage with one suitcase, with a white plastic bag with blue Hebrew lettering, which he handed to me. "These were Charlie's. I thought you might want them," he said. Inside the bag were Charlie's phylacteries in a red velvet pouch and a prayer book. The bag's Hebrew lettering surprised me in the humid savannah, this reminder of my Jerusalem life, and it took me a moment to pronounce the inscription, "Gitelman's Glatt Kosher Meats."

Daniel spied Patty and dropped his suitcase in the cottage's doorway. He maneuvered by me down the steps and strode across the clearing to her. Patty looked up from her baby scales as Daniel waded between the African mothers and crying babies to reach her. He wrapped his Ichabod Crane arms around her slender frame, and she hugged him back. They held each other a long time in the sticky afternoon.

For a moment, I blamed myself for Daniel's lost love. Why couldn't I have left the poor man alone? But then I noticed Pastor Allen slouching against the doorframe of the infirmary hut, watching Daniel hug his wife. Contrasted to his soldierly posture in the cemetery, this brave man seemed bowed now into an angle of despair, as if Patty, like Daniel, had also been unrepentant. I immediately chided myself for my remorse. What Daniel had done with Patty Allen was wrong—very wrong—and I shouldn't condone it. My cheeks warmed in shame then that I seemed to have lost all ability to distinguish right from wrong, and I gazed away from the pair like they were something pornographic.

Daniel ambled to me. His gray-blue eyes were wet and bloodshot. "Okay, let's go." He reached up the steps for his suitcase and started ahead of me to the clearing's edge where a path wove between baobab trees to the main dirt road where he turned right for the fourteen-kilometer hike to the Volta River and Ghana. His back was more curved than usual under the burden of his suitcase. His gray bangs bounced up and down on his head, like a toupee.

The rutted dirt road wound through yam fields and forded little streams. We passed farmers with yoked oxen and children strolling to school. I walked along next to Daniel, tall and no longer fat, in my uniform of Bermuda shorts, Hawaiian shirt, and thongs. My hair had grown past my ears; my nose was stuffed up from allergies and peeling from the sun. When I thought Daniel calmed down some, I traded luggage with him. I gave him Charlie's bag and hauled his valise on my head, like a coolie.

We walked in silence that first, muggy afternoon of our journey home. Both of us were still self-involved in the African world we were leaving, in the new lives we'd take up in Israel after a month of travel. We were trekking home overland, Daniel having even less money than myself. I didn't mind the prospect of a wearying, uneventful trip, though. It struck me as a good decompression period from Togo, a chance to sort through my issues without the violence of coups or religious disputations, the worry of what my next move should be.

A mammy wagon piled high with mattresses, burlap sacks of charcoal, and bleating goats stopped for us some miles after the mission. The African passengers crowded together on their bench seats to make room for us. Nobody spoke as the truck labored up and down the muddy road. We were like refugees fleeing a holocaust. Calypso music, then news, blared from the cab: the coup had been squelched; caches of arms were discovered in Lome; President Eyadema had instituted martial law.

The Volta River was torrid brown and littered with debris from the heavy rains. The British ferryboat banged against its splintered dock as the Togo douaniers shouted in French for mammy wagon passengers to line up on the steep gravelly decline to the river.

The officials examined passports in the approaching dusk, knifed open parcels, and emptied suitcases. The wagon, stripped of its passengers, headed back up the mission road. I worried my name might be on these gendarmes' wanted lists, especially since my visit with Raymont, and I repictured the coup d'etat bombs in Lome and dusty collapse of exploded buildings, the wild blaze of gasoline fires, packs of soldiers roving Lome's streets and beating civilians. The douaniers waved Daniel and me down to the ferry.

The boat strained across the thunderous river at dark. Uprooted trees and debris banged the boat's hull. Daniel and I steadied ourselves on the railing. The Togo shoreline dimmed to the soldiers' cooking fire; Ghana was a black horizon of river grass ahead.

The captain and his apprentices roped the ferry to its Ghana mooring and helped us to shore. A full yellow moon emerged from a sheath of rain clouds and lit up the raging river, then was hidden again. The band of river grass shimmered in a wet southern breeze.

A second mammy wagon and deserted customs booth waited for us beyond the ferry's dock—this cheered everyone. Mattresses, burlap sacks of charcoal, the bleating goats, were lashed to the new truck's roof. Soon, we were driving to

Tamale, and the African travelers chatted and laughed. The fugitive atmosphere of Togo evaporated, like we'd reached safe haven.

This feeling of relief, the sense of being delivered from the bowels of something foul, stayed with me to Tamale where we spent the night and through the next morning when Daniel and I caught a bush taxi north to Ougadougou, and even the next days after that when we reached Niamey, the lush savannah rainy season drying into the dust and heat of the Sahel.

From Niamey, Daniel and I bush-taxied northeast to Tahoua, In-Gall, then to Agadez where the Sahara began. We slept in grimy hovels and ate street food with Fulani, Bella, and Tuareg tribesmen, that great mix of nomadic and semi-nomadic tribes that had settled and caravaned through these tin-shack Sahelian towns. And still this good feeling of being delivered from something foul stayed with me. I described it to myself as a sense of moral progress, my perception of steady forward movement toward a desired goal. My uncle was good company, irreverent once away from the pastor, and funny, like the aging men in steam rooms at the YMCA, and my confusion from Daniel's sordid tale of his marriage to Vivian was washed away for the moment in the desert's gorgeous sunsets and dawns, in the sand and wide expanses of land and sky.

From Agadez, Daniel and I hitched to Arlit. We spent two nights in a filthy hotel before I found an Arab trucker headed north out of black Africa and who agreed for a decent price to take Daniel and me and feed us. The trucker's name was Yusef Fezzane, a stocky, mustached man in his late thirties who had a wife and three daughters in Langhouat, Algeria, and who drove semis of Yoruba cloth to Algiers for a consortium of Arab textile merchants. He was traveling north via Tamanrasset and Langhouat where he'd stop to see his family. Then he'd drive to Djelfa, nestled in the Atlas Mountains, and take the trip's last steep leg down to the Mediterranean, through Boukhari to Algiers. Yusef traced the route for us on a map. With the exception of a detour through Reggane, where

Carla Ernester stranded Charlie and me, it was the identical route we'd hitched on our original, fateful trek south.

And like the first trip, it took from dawn to dark to navigate the semipacked sand plains and scrub-tufted bluffs between Arlit, Niger, and the Algerian border town of Assamakka. When Yusef finally stopped for the night, Daniel and I were exhausted from troweling hot sand from the truck's stalled wheels and wedging sheet metal runners into the soft ground as a ramp for the truck to free itself. Yusef cooked us onions and couscous over a portable gas stove and gave us water to drink from rubber waterskins lashed to the truck's belly. He made us each a glass of heavily sugared Tuareg tea. Then he climbed into the cab to sleep, and Daniel and I camped outside in the dry cold air beneath the wide brilliant spread of stars, in cheap green sleeping bags that we'd bought in Niamey.

The following morning, we began the long climb to Tamanrasset through beds of sun-burnt igneous rock and dried up waddies. Our gravelly route steepened by the early afternoon as we reached the Ahaggar Mountains. A right side tire blew out near Tamanrasset. Yusef nursed his listing van to the oasis's high-altitude truck grounds. The flat and square grounds were crowded with other Arab trucks and the Jeeps of trans-Saharan tourists. Lines of laundry and pup tents stretched between these travelers' cars. The disheveled men and women, mostly French, circled small brush fires. They smoked Gauloises and held tin cups of black coffee. A pair of the men approached Yusef for a ride, but Yusef shook his head. He pried off the inner tube and instructed Daniel and me in his pidgin French to guard the truck while he walked to town for a new tire.

Daniel and I sat down on the hard ground. Each of us leaned against a wheel on opposite ends of the rig. My wheel was still warm from our day's journey, and I could smell its rubber. The truck grounds' left flank was bordered with scrub trees; its right tapered up to rocky mounds. Ahead of us, the drab land stretched out levelly to a precipitous end. It was how medieval Europeans might have imagined the end of the flat world to look: earth meeting sky in a thin brown line.

The daylight was dusky and blue. Daniel lit a stogie and blew smoke rings into the cooling air. The French tourists were camped to one side of him and I could smell their brush fires, Gauloises. Their laundry waved like flags in the dusty breeze. Their French sounded throaty and garbled, like Arabic. The sky darkened to navy blue, to black, as I leaned against the truck's warm tire, and gazed at the foggy swirl of the Milky Way. In my vision, the scraggly tourists dimmed to a campfire, like the Togo shoreline had. Daniel's stogie glowed red when he puffed. I could make out his smooth narrow face, his six-day whiskers then, his graying bangs. His cigar's acrid stink blended curiously well with the oasis's other smells of tire rubber and palm branch fires, the desert wind, which smelled like autumn leaves, as if the tobacco itself were natively grown.

"Isn't this lovely, Muz?" Daniel said cheerfully after a time. His head was cocked backward against Yusef's truck tire, to best see the stars.

"Certainly is," I agreed, but Daniel's too-casual tone bothered me, a tone that completely belied Charlie's death and his own expulsion from the mission. It was as if our desert voyage and his impending new life were only fresh incidents in a daily comic strip and not personal upheavals or significant results of his behavior or past events. And I was struck how Daniel regarded his own life as one vast moment of instantaneity, a blur of time that did not admit of responsibilities to others or moral consideration or choice—any karmic sense of cause and effect. In other words, I sensed that my uncle regretted nothing that he'd ever done, besides divorcing Vivian. And as Daniel deigned for the present to exercise his free will, he reminded me of what I might become forty years hence. I remembered my own sins then, in particular my father's abandonment. The shame of my decision that hot morning in Tanout warmed my cheeks again in this high-altitude oasis and squashed in one brief moment my whole perception of spiritual and bodily progress from Togo's bowels.

The cold Saharan winds whooshed through the truck grounds. Daniel's hair whipped about his forehead in the red glow of his stogie. I listened to the snap of laundry and the tourists' garbled French. I thought the yellow-red flames of their brush fire shaped like Charlie's goatee. Dread invaded my bowels and cramped my stomach, the awful realization that my desertion of Charlie would never leave me. I grew nauseated. I had to walk around Yusef's dusty truck and inhale deeply of the cold air. The whole flat truck grounds with its desolate landscape and rough people crystallized in my mind then as a physical manifestation of my lost soul: the chilly winds, the scraggly tourists with their knotted speech and ragged laundry, the scrub trees, Daniel as an older aimless Murray Orloff. And this horrified me. It was the megaton bomb reaction that I'd hoped for when I'd encouraged Daniel to tell me his sordid tale of my family's history, and it came as a repugnance against my relatives' ancient passions as the cause and effect of their unexamined lives. It's what I'd certainly become if I failed to direct my life—such a man leaned against a truck tire twenty feet east of me. Yet my horror was also built upon the series of decisions I'd taken to resolve my cowardice toward Charlie—accepting Ruth's offer to deliver the coup d'etat money, my refusal to reveal Raymont's whereabouts to Mr. Fitzwater, stopping my theological disputation with Pastor Allen and apologizing to Daniel on Charlie's behalf. I never wanted to backslide again.

But I had a powerful, frightened clarity on this dark, cold evening, and the memory of my past decisions and present distaste at Daniel and Vivian's marriage converged in my mind as unconscious but articulate steps back toward Charlie's religious beliefs. I sat still and listened to the French tourists' speech and smelled their Gauloises as I watched the Arab truck drivers huddle around a palm fire and swig on contraband Johnny Walker Scotch—this vivid hallucination of the rot of my soul—and I understood my reflective thought and decisions as rational, subconscious efforts to reconstruct the religious formality of my mind. The great irony was that the very thing that stranded me in Togo—Charlie's lie— should be the principal influence that brought me ideologically home. The same misguided Charlie who wrenched me from yeshiva for this tragic journey was also the religious visionary who had furnished me with the talmudic education to rescue myself.

And this strong whiff of my almost a priori future decay was potent enough to weaken my combative attitude toward my religious background. It was as if practically, like instructions to a model kit, the only way to avoid searing memories of my cowardice was to build such guilt into life change. And as I leaned against Yusef Fezzane's truck on this chilly Saharan night, I began a monologue to my uncle about Israel and what he could expect there, but also a monologue about Judaism, the religion that was the germ of his dead brother's life, a monologue that evolved to classic proofs of the existence of God and literal truth of the Torah.

My monologue continued throughout the next morning and the next day after that as Yusef drove us down out of Tamanrasset to the sandy wind-stippled plains near In-Salah, where scattered thorny shrub bushes and palm trees grew from cinnamon-colored earth. Over the plaintive taped wailing of Yusef's Arab music, as the truck alternately raced then lurched over the rough plains, I spoke to my uncle about how every decision in life was based on odds and that nothing was ever a hundred percent sure. In the absence of this surety, I argued, human beings made life decisions by gathering and weighing information, by considering the consequences of their choices and making educated guesses based on the odds. In other words, the decision to be religious, in principle, should be no different than the decision to buy a Toyota over a Chevrolet. Since a person didn't require a hundred percent proof that Toyotas were better cars than Chevrolets before he actually bought a model, one hundred percent proof of God's existence wasn't necessary or responsible of him to expect because he didn't conduct *any* of the rest of his life like that.

Daniel said, nodding, "I hear that."

We were holed up in Fort Miribel in the central Sahara because of a sandstorm. Our desert hovel was dark, grimy, and cool. Gusts of sand smacked the mud and stone walls as I talked next about the millions of people alive today who believed in the Old Testament's miracles as literally written and how these people acquired their beliefs from their parents and their parents from their parents, a chain of belief extending back to the three million Hebrew slaves who fled Egypt. The obvious question, I asked my uncle then, was how did this chain of belief get started? Specifically, I mentioned the miracle of the manna and how it fell from heaven every day except the Sabbath for forty years. I rebutted the possibility that one person or a group of people could have duped a whole nation into believing such a public event if it never in fact occurred. Such a claim was completely without historical parallel. The manna, in short, had to have been real. Which then lent credence to the rest of the Old Testament text. And after two more days of sandstorm in Fort Miribel, after a hot day's drive to Berriane, I concluded my monologue with a description of the Jews' two thousand years of continuous persecution and exile, how it had all been an exact prediction by the Jewish prophets, and how the Almighty promised to return the Jews to the land of Israel and—behold!—Daniel could see that we're there.

But Daniel remained unimpressed by my arguments, just like in the mission cemetery. Perhaps after my debate with the pastor he simply wasn't ready to entertain a new theology. Perhaps, as I said, ideas didn't compel him like they had Charlie. Yet while Daniel gummed his stogie and only half listened to my monologue, as we trucked through the northern Sahara's desolate waste, past the oxidized wrecks of burned and abandoned cars, past the tiny brown oases that sprouted like mushrooms from the scalded brown desert floor, my arguments began to convince me.

And it was only in Langhouat, when Yusef stopped for a day to see his wife and daughters, as I watched his youngest girl tug his thick brown mustache and bow down on the floor with him when he prayed, that I understood I'd allowed myself extra receptivity to believe in the Torah's divinity because of family pressure. What would my mother, siblings, friends, and rabbis say if I came home nonreligious? Yet I didn't deem this a negative. I recognized that based solely on Socratic reflection I would never recommit to my father's orthodoxy. Rather, I needed the sight of Yusef Fezzane dandling his little girls and the serious, practical questions this raised in order for me to take my own monologue seriously. What kind of relationship did I want to have with my wife? How could I best raise my kids? How did I wish to grow old and die?

And as we trucked out of Langhouat for the steep, grinding climb into the Atlas Mountains, I knew that my theological conclusions were solid enough for me to become Orthodox again. Still, I remarked to myself, I'd known these proofs all along. What was different now? Even the nagging worry that I could be a bastard, that ugly threat of social leprosy Daniel's family history raised, wasn't enough to steer me away. I understood its possibility only as a test of my resolve. Would I have, as I once heard someone in Pittsfield say about Charlie, lots of guts? My answer to "What was different now?" came the following dawn in the Atlas Mountains.

Yusef's truck strained us out of the brown, oceanlike Sahara and we stopped for the evening at Ksar el Boukhari, one day south of Algiers, in a truck grounds with pine trees that cracked in the moist Mediterranean wind. Why the proofs convinced me now became obvious to me, a result of my past five jaded months: it was impossible to be a Jew unless you were first a mensch. And it was impossible to be a mensch without both divine and human obligations, a grand and studied selflessness, a hard-headed pursuit of truth. Without forcing your love to overcome your hate.

The answer to my "lots of guts" question occurred after these ruminations, in the beautiful, cold, and lonely orange dawn, when I forced myself out of my cheap green sleeping bag to stand up in the damp mountain air. I hopped up and down for warmth and rinsed my hands and face with water from the rubber waterskins lashed to Yusef's truck. I grabbed the Gitelman's Glatt Kosher Meats bag and strode to the far corner of the truck ground, into a stand of pine trees where I wouldn't be seen. The trees smelled fresh and sweet in the Mediterranean wind and they bent and swayed around me, like old Jews. I pulled Charlie's phylacteries from their velvet pouch: one small black box with straps for my left arm and one small box to affix to my head, like a laurel wreath. I slid the loop of the arm phylactery up my bicep and positioned it just above my elbow. I chanted the proper blessing and wrapped the strap down over my forearm. I tightened the head phylactery over my long hair. And with fresh sorrow at my father's death and wonder at the lovely rightness of this moment, I faced Jerusalem to give thanks to the Almighty for His salvation from great darkness and to petition Him for future help, to pray for the repose of Charlie Orloff's soul.

TWELVE

My moment of grace passed as it must and left me feeling tender and raw, like I'd wept. I wanted my mother's comfort now and not the crack of the truck stop's pines in the damp Mediterranean wind or the dawn's orange glow. It was the company of familiar people and objects, the Hebrew language, Judaism, and familiar place names that I craved in my sudden, almost sexual urge to return home. The sight of my mother smoking a Kool inside the walls of our cramped Old City apartment and her cantaloupe lipstick, the wrinkles that played about her mouth when she inhaled, the scarf that covered her gray-blond hair, her tall slender frame.

I wrapped up Charlie's phylacteries, replaced them in the bag, and strolled back to Yusef Fezzane's truck. Soon Yusef woke, then Daniel. We drove north from Ksar el Boukhari through Medea where the Atlas Mountains sloped steeply toward the sea, and Blida where we halted for coffee and pita sandwiches. We drove another hour on paved road before we spotted Algiers, a white skyline against an india ink sea, and then closer, columns of square concrete buildings terraced onto semicircles of hills.

Yusef dropped Daniel and me at the railway station where we'd take a train to Tunisia and then boat home. Daniel shook hands with Yusef and then Yusef with me. Our drive across the Sahara had been long and mercifully uneventful enough for me to work out my religious issues and I was thankful for that. I'd miss Yusef Fezzane, his almond eyes and heavy brown mustache, the sight of his youngest daughter bowing with him in prayer. He left my uncle and me underneath the brick eave of the old colonial train station, and we waved to him as he climbed into his dusty truck, even as he pulled away from us for the drive to his cloth warehouse.

Inside the hangarlike station, Daniel and I purchased sleeping berths for the overnight trip to Tunis. Our compartment was chilly and urine stenched, like with Charlie, its windows dirty and cracked. The station seemed like a huge yawning mouth and our train its tongue as we pulled away from Algiers in the purple dusk. There was a glimpse of the dark sea, low pier buildings, crates and winches on metal docks, oil tankers motionless on an azure horizon. The concentrated yellow lights of the city thinned at its outskirts, and soon we were racing in the valleys between the brittle peaks of this northeast flank of the Atlas range. The mountains looked fractured yet arranged in the near dark, a succession of cubist noses.

Daniel sat across from me in our smelly compartment and stared out of the window and frowned. Perhaps he was thinking of Rachael or his marriage to Vivian. His hands were folded in his lap and our knees touched as the train rattled through a rough switch in a mountain village. Cold air leaked through window cracks as the fluorescent light in our berth flickered on and off. Daniel and I talked sporadically and only of travel connections, each of us again involved with our recent and further pasts, with the lives we'd take up in Israel soon. Later on, the squat Arab conductor slipped into the compartment and unfolded our beds from the wall. He furnished us with stained sheets and blankets with moth holes and tugged down the window shade and the shade to the corridor. He wished us good night.

Daniel and I climbed into the bunks but kept our clothes on. I listened to other passengers pace the hall outside our berth, their Arabic harsh sounding, like the clack of the train wheels against the tracks. Daniel quickly fell asleep, and snored.

I lay awake a long time in the cold night as our cracked window rattled in its frame. I tried to distinguish the train's bad smells—urine, grease, whisky, hair oil, damp sheepskin coats—and became aware in my fastidious addition of smells that the tenderness I experienced after my moment of grace had blown up into a palpable fright about the bastard issue and what the confrontation between my mother and Daniel might unearth. It is impossible to overemphasize the disastrous social consequences of this stigma, and I perceived my nervousness, notwithstanding my previous consideration of it as only a test of my resolve, as something that could potentially wedge me away from my newfound belief. I might even continue to think Jewish theology to be true, but who needed such aggravation? It would be easier for me to become secular again, emigrate to New York like so many other Israelis, and find a job. After all, I had an American passport.

Which is when I understood that my nervousness in the Tunis train was similar to my journey to Daniel's mission when I was afraid of meeting Charlie and being confronted with my cowardice and irreligiosity. I had, nevertheless, tramped north to meet him anyway. Here, too, I knew that I needed to endure this bastard fear that chafed against my religious commitment, like sackcloth. Tests of belief would come at me in various forms all my life, maybe in the form of a difficult job or piece of Bible criticism, maybe poverty, God forbid. Such a realization changed my theological understanding of my African experience. No longer was the Dark Continent a necessary entropy to my religious sensibility. Rather, it was merely a test of those beliefs and emblematic of all religious conflicts that I'd confront in my life. And while these tests had the power to wedge me away from Judaism, they also had the power, if transcended, to become the very reasons I stayed Orthodox. Which is why I decided upon my rearrival in Israel to return to the semiascetic life of the yeshiva. I understood only too well how I needed to reimmerse myself in the tradition to reconstruct my religiosity and thereby escape modernity's debilitating effects. I needed, in other words, to find out all over again how to be a Jew.

But such good strategy as regards life's tests doesn't abate worry, and the closer Daniel and I traveled to Israel the more my fear gripped me: from our train ride to Tunis and overnight ferry to Palermo, to our three-day boat trip across the Mediterranean to Haifa port, the bus ride from Haifa to Tel Aviv and up the bleak Judean hills to Jerusalem.

Yet it was only longing and not fear I felt that rainy Thursday noon in April 1981, just after my twenty-fourth birthday, when Daniel and I alighted from our taxi outside Jaffa Gate in the Old City. I only wanted to hug my mother and Louise and Max very hard and comfort them about Charlie's death. I didn't care that moment about my long hair or scraggly beard, my dirty Hawaiian shirt and Bermuda shorts, that Vivian would be alarmed at how much thinner I'd become, or Daniel and his confused hopes. I just wanted my family. And as we marched through the Arab souk, the booths of brass trinkets, pastry stands, tailor shops, the coffee brewers, falafel joints, and loaded donkeys, the Arabs in kaffiyehs, tourists, and Israeli soldiers, the black-coated religious Jews— everything seemed only cardboard props in my rush toward my mom.

I turned right at a littered crossroads in the souk. Daniel followed me out of the Arab market, up cobbled steps to Misgav Ladach, the main walkway of the Old City's Jewish Quarter. A narrow promenade on my left opened to a view of the Wall. In the warm drizzle, the mammoth blocks were darker than their usual yellow-beige and I noticed that no one prayed. But I didn't want to linger over the view now and hurried up Misgav Ladach, taking another right at a tourist kiosk farther along, walking quickly by a row of Judaica shops to the branch post office where my mother worked. I didn't look around to see if Daniel kept step with me but rushed past the post office's glass doors.

My mother stood behind a Formica counter. She glanced up when I dropped Daniel's bag but didn't recognize me. She looked back at a sheet of stamps she was counting out for a young soldier in patrol fatigues. Her drab green dress and faded yellow headscarf, her unpainted lips made her appear older and more careworn than her fifty years, like the Sephardi women who begged coins at the Wailing Wall—it was really her.

I stood unrecognized and wet in the corner and stared at my mother. My heart beat wildly as I remembered the office's white plasterboard walls and stone floor, its gunmetal book-cases behind the counter, which held the brown parcels, my mother's choppy immigrant Hebrew, the husky cigarette rasp of her voice as she sold stamps. And I imagine it was my heavy breathing that made her look up again but peer at me more closely, as if to assure herself that I wasn't someone bad.

"It's me, Mom."

My mother craned her neck forward and squinted at me. The young soldier kept count of the stamps, "Sixteen, seventeen . . ."

"Muz?"

I stepped over Daniel's suitcase. I ducked beneath the office's Formica counter and stood up on its far side. My mother gripped my biceps. She cocked her head backward to take me in. She gasped when she was sure it was me and pitched herself forward onto my chest.

My eyes heated up and teared. I held her tight. "Missed you, Ma." I felt her shoulder blades and the moist tip of her nose on my neck. She rubbed my back up and down, but roughly, desperately, like she hadn't ever expected to see me again.

"Murray," she cried. "Murray."

"I'm so sorry about Charlie, Ma." I wept.

"There there," she said, to comfort us both. "There there."

We rocked back and forth beneath the post office's neon lights, in its paint and sawdust smells, as the soldier watched us and held his stamps.

Then my mother froze in my arms. She loosened her grip on me. "God have mercy on us!"

I turned around. Daniel stood tall and humpbacked in the doorway and he chomped on a stogie. His pince-nez were clamped to the end of his nose and his olive poncho was slick from the drizzle, like an aging desperado from a B-rated cowboy movie.

"Hello, Viv. How the hell are you?" He was loud and cocky, a seducer full of the memory of their first meeting at Avaloch. Here, though, he sounded just plain bizarre. His voice was manic when he should have been demure. It was all the more galling since this moment Mother and I mourned Charlie. But Daniel was a wildly unpredictable man, and what did I expect? And while I felt bad for my mom—she was obviously frightened by her ex-husband's grizzled features—the instant, powerful tension between them was the very confrontation I'd hoped for to determine truthfully whether I was a bastard or not.

The tension increased yet again when Vivian said flatly, "Hello, Dan," as she struggled to be cordial within the social confines of having the soldier and me present, as if she didn't think that I knew about their marriage.

Daniel asked, "Is that all you have to say to me, Viv?"

Stress flushed my mother's face red. Her hands dropped from my biceps. "Please, one moment," she said, and finished with the soldier at the counter. As the man left the office, Mother said, "Okay, I'll take my lunch break now." She grabbed an umbrella and hung a Hebrew and English placard in the glass doorway, then locked the office's glass doors.

Daniel and I followed her at a distance in single file, like a guerrilla patrol. We walked past the Judaica shops and a group of German tourists with cameras and rain hats. We passed by the children's school and ritual bath, the side streets where my friends lived, and through our own cobblestone courtyard—familiar sights and yet strange from my months away, all unfocused images against the anxiety that now infected us all.

Mother fumbled with the key to our apartment door and finally opened the lock. Daniel and I trailed her into the small dining room, where I dropped Daniel's bag. She asked us to sit at the rectangular dinner table, like I was a stranger also, and retreated to the kitchen. Daniel, turned sullen from Vivian's chilly greeting, sat deathly still in his poncho.

Our cramped apartment seemed unchanged except for a web of tan moisture stains on the room's eastern wall. Otherwise, it was the same scuffed tile floor and dilapidated furniture, the same shelves of Hebrew books and kitsch painting of dancing Hassidim near the front entrance.

Mother returned from the kitchen with a plate of vanilla wafers, glasses, and refrigerated seltzer. She mentioned that

Max was in yeshiva and Louise was at university—her attempt at pleasantries. But Vivian's skin remained flushed and tightly drawn across her cheeks and belied her chitchat. I knew the look: the same expression she wore in department stores before she yelled at the manager.

She paced beneath the moisture stains on the room's far wall, working up to whatever she wished to announce. I poured seltzer for Daniel and myself. I bit into a creamy sweet cookie and waited for Vivian to speak.

Her hands circled as she paced, gestures that bespoke of her confusion of where to begin to describe the enormity of what needed to be talked out. I noticed her fingers were red and chapped like they'd been in Monsey when she developed an allergy to the tap water and had to slaver medicated cream on them and wear white cotton gloves to sleep. Presently, I took this ruin of her hands as a nervous symptom of her grief for Charlie.

Then, as if she decided to chuck diplomacy, as if she understood that there was no painless way to speak of the ancient things that marred hers and Daniel's lives, Mother stopped her pacing and gazed at Daniel. She pointed a forefinger at him, and said, "I'm mad you came back here, Dan. And, Muz, I'm mad that you brought him back."

"But Charlie—" I protested.

"Charlie was wrong!" Mother snapped, her lips twitching in anger as she glared at me, then at Daniel. "What did you imagine, Dan? Charlie's dead so you and I will get back together?"

Daniel looked away from scornful Vivian. His poncho crinkled as he turned his glass in the gray noon light, as he watched the seltzer bubbles rise and burst.

"Charlie said that he wanted to bring you to Israel so you could live as a Jew," Mother continued in a quieter but still angry tone. She stopped her pacing and stood framed in the apartment window. "Though I believe the real point was simply to see you again and apologize for everything that happened."

"We never met," Daniel informed her in a whisper.

"But Charlie's dead now," Vivian went on. "And I just

don't want you around, Dan. Do you understand that? I want you out of here when I go back to work after lunch. Murray, you'll take your uncle to a hotel or a youth hostel this afternoon."

And in that long moment before my uncle nodded his acceptance of my mother's decree, which banished him forever from her life, a nod that would be an emotional recognition that he was a plague to her and symbol of all that had been chaotic and wrong with her past, I decided not to tell her about Charlie's lie nor my cowardice toward him. Since she'd come to grips with Father's death as the unfortunate result of his momentary, poor judgment and not as any dramatic consequence of a tragic character flaw, what was to be gained if I shattered what must have been her fragile mental peace with other ruinous details?

More pressing now, though, was this bastard issue. I found the proper moment to broach the subject when Mother stepped away from the window and fiddled with a paperweight on a shelf, when she wished to show that the meeting had ended. I deemed this the correct time and asked, "How did you and Daniel get married, Mom?"

"We had a reform wedding—not an Orthodox one—and Rav Eliyahu told Charlie and me that everything was all right," she answered immediately, understanding my worry, meaning that the union between Daniel and her was like man and mistress according to Jewish law and not like man and wife, which would have brought us Leviticus bastard problems: it was like Charlie marrying his brother's ex-girlfriend.

It was all Mother needed to say—I knew that Reform rabbis had no power of Jewish law. More important, I could check out her story with Rav Eliyahu and would. I felt enormously relieved but remained curious how Charlie and she rationalized their marriage and their kids' status until we moved to Israel and met Rav Eliyahu. I asked her this.

"We didn't know there was a problem until we moved to Cleveland," she said. "And when Charlie found out just how big a problem it was, he moved us to Phoenix. I thought it was the end of our Judaism."

"But what happened? He got brave again and we moved to Israel?"

"He didn't want Louise to marry Manuel Garcia. This alone brought him back to religion."

"But the point is that he lost his nerve but got it back," I insisted, "even though—"

"Even though what?" Vivian asked.

"Even though he passed away," I said, really meaning, even though Charlie lost his nerve a second, fatal time. For my mother's disclosure, making Charlie twice a coward, once in Cleveland and once in Jerusalem, proved my final epiphany: that while Rav Eliyahu answered Charlie favorably concerning his marriage to Vivian and his kids' status, the experience of asking life-affecting questions of law so unnerved my father, the awful vulnerability that his life rested completely in the rav's hands, that he couldn't approach the question of law that needed to be asked about our trek to Africa with the same willingness to listen as he once had. Hence, Charlie's lie. Hence, our trip to Africa where he died. And it was with this dual sense of my father as an unusually brave but mistake-prone man and also as a visionary who was the architect of my own redemption from myself, that my uncle's meeting with my mother ground to an end. Daniel finally nodded acceptance of my mother's harsh will. Mother said she had to return to work. Daniel and I stood up. Mother opened the apartment door to let us out.

And once again we walked on the Old City's cobblestone alleys. The drizzle had stopped, and charcoal clouds raced through an overcast sky. Vivian marched ahead of us, then humpbacked Daniel, then me. Mother halted at the turn to the post office, near the steps to the Wailing Wall. "I'll have dinner ready by six, Muz," she informed me, and then she turned to Daniel. "Good luck to you, Dan. I hope the rest of your life goes well for you." Then she walked around the corner, forever gone from his life.

Daniel stood still, his back to me. After a moment, he swiveled around. He wore his poncho and chewed on his stogie. He stared at me over the blue frames of his pince-nez. Slowly, slowly, he raised his arms from his sides in a giant shrug, like a huge green-winged bird about to take to flight. "What now, Murray?" he asked me forlornly. "What now?"

Rain clouds cast the air about us gray. Yeshiva students carrying Talmuds walked past us, besides a group of blond Swedish tourists, a pair of Arab construction workers pushing wheelbarrows, children on tricycles. Uncle Daniel stood in the middle of the cobbled walkway, arms lifted above his shoulders in a huge green shrug, and I remembered my trip with Charlie and how I'd depended on him. I'd told my uncle in Africa that I loved him; it was time to start meaning it. But, mostly, I reflected that since I'd completed Charlie's mission I *was* Charlie as far as my uncle was concerned. Which meant that I couldn't simply deliver him to the bus stop, wish him well like my mother, and be rid of him. It meant, unless he skipped the country, that I'd always—somehow—be responsible for him. Thus Uncle Daniel became the final legacy of my travels with Charlie. But that was all right— I could accept that responsibility. And in accepting that responsibility I figured out what to do.

"Well, how about we first go visit the Wall?" And I picked up his suitcase. I led him down the stone steps of the Jewish Quarter and through its security checkpoint, past the number one bus stop and across the white stone plaza to the Wall. I grabbed two cardboard skullcaps from a box kept for tourists and nudged Daniel forward toward the huge beige blocks of the remains of Solomon's temple to God.

White birds circled above us. The sun was a yellow smudge in the dark clouds. There were particular fissures in the Wall I remembered, and bullet holes from old wars, tufts of weeds, birds' nests, the great stones' chilly touch. First, I gathered a minyan from the beggars and tourists and led the afternoon prayers and said kaddish for Charlie. Afterward, a yeshiva boy lent me a pencil and paper, and Daniel and I took turns writing letters to God, as is the custom of pilgrims. And when, not so many years later, I married a nice Sephardi girl and had a bunch of kids (I finally left yeshiva and became a mohel, slicing foreskins, bringing new souls into the bris; Louise became an internist; Max a rabbi; Mother never remarried; Daniel stayed irreligious and moved to Tel Aviv where he worked as an appliance repairman and married a Hungarian widow), when I had my kids and loved them well I thought back to the sharp clarity of this day because it was when I finally—finally!—came to love my uncle. It was when I realized that love was a lot of work and not always sincere and that showing love to family when you didn't feel like it was an obligation. And I always remembered the drizzle and wind that made us shiver, the sun, swirling birds, and slate clouds, how I put my arm around Daniel and watched him write, how I folded our letters together when we finished and stuffed them hard into a crack in the Wall, along with all the other notes, as far as my long fingers would reach.